8543

DATE DUE			

Following My Own Footsteps

MARY DOWNING HAHN'S many Avon Camelot novels include *Stepping on the Cracks,* which received the Scott O'Dell Award for Historical Fiction and was an ALA Notable Book. Among her most recent books are *The Wind Blows Backward,* an ALA Best Book for Young Adults; *The Gentleman Outlaw and Me—Eli;* and *Look For Me by Moonlight.*
She and her husband, Norm, live in Columbia, Maryland.

Avon Books are available at special quantity discounts for bulk purchases for sales promotions, premiums, fund raising or educational use. Special books, or book excerpts, can also be created to fit specific needs.

For details write or telephone the office of the Director of Special Markets, Avon Books, Inc., Dept. FP, 1350 Avenue of the Americas, New York, New York 10019, 1-800-238-0658.

Following My Own Footsteps

Mary Downing Hahn

AN AVON CAMELOT BOOK

AVON BOOKS, INC.
1350 Avenue of the Americas
New York, New York 10019

Copyright © 1996 by Mary Downing Hahn
Published by arrangement with Clarion Books, an imprint of Houghton Mifflin
Company
Library of Congress Catalog Card Number: 95-50144
ISBN: 0-380-72990-3
RL: 4.8
www.avonbooks.com

First Avon Camelot Printing: April 1998

CAMELOT TRADEMARK REG. U.S. PAT. OFF. AND IN OTHER COUNTRIES, MARCA REGISTRADA,
HECHO EN U.S.A.

Printed in the U.S.A.

OPM 10 9 8 7 6 5 4 3

One

✧ ✧ ✧ ✧ ✧ ✧ ✧ ✧ ✧

"Mama," I said, letting my voice rise higher than the wind in the treetops, "Mama, come on, hurry up. I hear the train!"

I tugged at her coat sleeve, trying to pull her along. If we missed the morning train, Mama might change her mind before the next one came. Instead of leaving, she'd head back home, if you can call it that, and wait for the cops to let the old man go. She'd forgive him. After all the evil he'd done to us, she'd take him back. And we'd be stuck forever down at the end of Davis Road. We'd never get out of College Hill. Never get away from the old man.

"Let go of me, Gordy," Mama said, shaking free of me. "Leave me be. We have plenty of time." She was carrying my littlest brother Bobby and towing Ernie by the hand. Victor lagged behind all of us, struggling to carry a grocery bag stuffed with his belongings.

"Wait for me," he whined every step of the way and

of course Mama did, standing there on the muddy road, her coat blowing open in the cold February wind. Not even telling Victor to get a move on. Just waiting as still as a statue.

"The train's blowing for the Berwyn crossing," I said. "College Hill's next and we still got four blocks to go."

My little sister June ran to the edge of the railroad bank and peered down the track. "It's coming, Mama, it's coming," she shrieked. "I see the smoke!"

"Wait, wait, don't go without me!" Victor ran toward us, trying to catch up. His old teddy bear bounced out of the sack and splashed into a mud puddle.

As quick as I could, I grabbed the bear and wiped him on my jacket. "Don't start crying, Victor, not now," I said. "We don't have time for the weeping willies."

He was already sniffling but I took his hand and dragged him toward the train station. "Choo-choo's coming, Victor!"

That cheered him up a bit, even made him walk a little faster. He'd been wanting to ride a train all his life. For that matter, so had I. I used to lie in bed at night, listening to the old man rant and rave in the living room, and daydream about hopping one of the freights that thundered by the house.

On really bad nights, I'd sneak out the bedroom window and walk down to the railroad tracks. Safe from the old man's fists, I'd sit in a tree and watch the trains go by. In the dark, the locomotives were a gorgeous sight, shooting sparks like dragons and hiding the stars with smoke. They roared and rumbled, making the rails bounce under their weight, and their whistles just about split the sky in half. Only trouble was, they went by too fast for me to grab hold of a boxcar and jump on the way hoboes do.

After a train passed, I'd sit there all by my lonesome, listening to the whistle blow for the next crossing and wondering where the train was going—New York, Detroit, Chicago, maybe out west to California and the redwood forest. Or down south to the Gulf Stream waters, like that song we sang in school.

I never sang with the other kids, of course. While they bellowed, I just sat there drawing Nazi bombers and stuff, but deep in my heart I knew all the words. And what they meant. Someday I, Gordon P. Smith, planned to travel that ribbon of highway under the endless skyway. I'd roam and ramble and follow my own footsteps, I'd leave all those snobby College Hill kids and teachers in the boring Maryland dust and never look back.

But in real life, things don't happen the way you imagine. Instead of heading west by myself, I was going to North Carolina on an ordinary old passenger train with my family. Or what was left of it. As I've said, the old man was in jail where, if you ask me, he'd belonged for years. My brother Donny was overseas fighting the Nazis and my brother Stuart was in an army hospital. That left Mama, June, and my three little brothers. June was six and not too bad for a girl. Victor was four, Ernie was three, and Bobby was two.

They reminded me of puppies nobody'd bothered to train. In fact, Bobby wasn't even housebroken yet.

"Hurry, hurry!" June hollered. "The train's almost here, Mama!"

Mama didn't walk a bit faster. If anything she was slowing down, looking behind her every now and then as if she expected to see the old man coming after us.

June ran ahead, her skinny legs scissoring as she jumped mud puddles. She clutched her grocery bag so tight her dolly's head bounced up and down like a rubber ball. "I'll tell the train to wait for you," she yelled.

Like me, June wanted to get out of town before the old man found us. He'd be mad as hell, that's for sure. No matter what evil things he'd done before, nobody had called the cops, he'd never gone to jail. He'd just slept it off and then begged Mama to forgive him.

"I'll never drink another drop, Ginny," he'd say, all weepy and smelly and bleary-eyed, ugly as sin and no more believable than the devil himself.

But Mama would forgive him. Her black eye would fade to purple and green and yellow and then clean away, she'd use the perfume he gave her, she'd smile again. "You see, Gordy," she'd say. "This time your father means it. No more whiskey."

A month or so would pass, and then one night he'd come home grinning that lopsided grin and walking like the floor tilted under his feet. Somebody would say the wrong thing or look at him funny and he'd be slapping us around all over again.

I took Mama's arm to hurry her. She winced, and I

let go, knowing I must have squeezed a sore place. "Let me carry Bobby," I said. "You can't handle him and that suitcase."

Bobby started wailing when I took him. Paying him no mind, I hurried to catch up with June. I knew for a fact Mama wouldn't let me get on the train with her baby unless she was with us.

Sure enough, when the locomotive came to a big steaming, huffing stop at the College Hill station, Mama climbed aboard just behind me. At last, I thought, we're getting out of town, just like a gang of outlaws leaving on a stagecoach. If any of my old enemies had been around, I'm sure they'd have cheered to see me go. But they were all in school, sitting in Wagner's room, looking at my empty desk and wondering when I'd be back.

"Never," I muttered as the train gave a jerk and started to move. "Never!"

Two

❖　❖　❖　❖　❖　❖　❖　❖　❖

B ecause of the war, the passenger car was jam-packed with soldiers and sailors. You can bet nobody looked happy to see us coming down the aisle. Mama had taken Bobby from me, and she was having trouble managing him and her big old suitcase. Ernie was hanging on to her leg, kind of bouncing along behind her and crying, of course. The rest of us followed like baby ducks, toting our grocery bags.

Somehow June and I managed to squeeze into a seat beside a fat lady who took up more than her share of space and sighed loudly when we sat down. Which is how most people react to our family. Just let us Smiths appear in public and the rest of the world curls up its toes and dies. Nobody likes us, not even strangers.

Anyhow, June and I were scrunched together so tight we couldn't breathe without poking each other. To make things worse, Victor sat on my lap, whining and wiggling and fussing. Across the aisle, Mama held Ernie on one knee and Bobby on the other, getting dirty looks from the soldier next to her.

Well, maybe I wouldn't have wanted to be sitting next to Mama, either. Even from my seat I could smell the load in Bobby's pants. Seemed like that kid wasn't ever going to learn to use a toilet.

After a few minutes, June tugged my arm. "Did Donny look like those soldiers when he left for the war, Gordy?"

I glanced at the guys she was pointing at. Most of them were talking loud and laughing even louder, wisecracking and telling jokes and smoking cigarettes till the air was so thick you could hardly breathe.

"Yeah," I said to June. "Donny looked just like them. Don't you remember?"

"He was tall," she said, frowning as if it was hard to recall even that much.

"Well, you were only about three when he left, not as big as Victor here." I nodded at my brother who was, thank the Lord, asleep. It struck me June wouldn't remember what Donny looked like if he got killed before the war was over. Neither would Victor or Ernie or Bobby. I was the only one besides Stu who'd remember him.

"Are they going to the war?" June asked, staring at the soldiers. "Are they going to fight Hitler like Donny?"

"Probably." I studied the soldiers again. Not all of them were joking and carrying on. Some of them sat by themselves, their noses pressed to the window like they were hoping to see a sign saying Hitler was dead, the war was over, they could go back home. They reminded me of Stu.

I looked at my sister, but she seemed to have lost interest in the soldiers. Pulling her dolly, a nearly bald, one-eyed wonder, out of her bag, she held it up so it could see out the window. "You're on the choo-choo train, Baby. We're going to Grandma's house."

June rocked the dolly and began singing, "'Over the river and through the woods to Grandmother's house we go.'"

The fat lady glanced at June and actually smiled. "I bet you love your granny, don't you?" she asked in one of those sugary-sweet voices grown-ups use when they speak to little kids like June.

June stopped singing and stared at the fat lady, who looked like a granny in a picture book. "I hope I love her," she said. "I didn't even know I had a grandma till Daddy went to jail and Mama called her on the phone and she said we could stay with her for a while."

The fat lady drew in her breath. "I see," she said, shifting a little closer to the window.

"Daddy got drunk. He beat up Mama and almost killed my brother Stu," June said as if it was something to brag about. "Daddy was mad 'cause Stu deserted from the army. Now Stu's in the hospital and Daddy's in jail and we're going over the river and through the woods to Grandma's house."

All the time June was babbling our family secrets, I was pinching her arm to shut her up. Finally she stopped talking and slapped my hand. "Quit that, Gordy!" To the fat lady she said, "I hope my daddy stays in jail forever and ever. He's a bad man and I hate him. Gordy hates him too."

The fat lady heaved herself to her feet and smoothed her dress. Clutching her purse, she began to inch past us toward the aisle.

"Are you going to the bathroom?" June asked. "Want us to save your place till you come back?"

Murmuring something about getting off the train at the next stop, the fat lady forced her way up the aisle, whacking a few soldiers with the suitcase she pulled down from the luggage rack.

"She was a nice lady," June said when the fat lady was gone.

"Why did you tell her about the old man?" I asked. "For the Lord's sake, June, there's no sense telling strangers your daddy's in jail."

"It was all I could think of to say." Spitting on her finger, June began cleaning her dolly's face. "Baby, you're all dirty! How often have I told you not to play in the mud?" She shook the doll so hard her head almost fell off. "Bad, bad Baby!"

I leaned back in my seat. Now that the fat lady was gone, I could actually see out the window. We'd passed through Washington while June was telling the whole train about the old man's current address, so I figured we must be in Virginia now. At first, the scenery looked pretty much the same as Maryland. Woods, still bare and brown from winter. A farm every now and then.

Horses running from the train. Cows standing around looking bored. Towns, houses, churches, schools, playgrounds.

It was warm and stuffy in the car, and I kept dozing off only to wake up every time the train stopped, which was pretty often. I hadn't slept very well the night before. I'd been scared to close my eyes for fear the old man would come home and start beating on us again. Kept seeing his ugly face, feeling his fists, hearing his voice cursing Stu, cursing Mama, cursing all of us, even Bobby who'd never done anything except get born.

"SOB," I muttered, clenching my own fists. "Hit me again and I'll kill you, I swear I will."

Beside me, June gave a little jump in her sleep. "Don't," she mumbled. "Don't."

I picked up poor old Baby, who'd tumbled to the floor, and laid her beside my sister. Trying to stay awake, I pressed my face against the cold window and watched the farmland streak past. Far away and blue against the sky I saw mountains, the first I'd ever seen. There was no snow on the tops, but they were taller than the hills I was used to.

It struck me this was the farthest I'd ever traveled in my whole entire life. The world seemed bigger here, not so closed in by fences and hedges and houses. The words of that song floated through my head again— the ribbon of highway, the endless skyway, the golden valley, the diamond desert. At last, I was beginning to roam and ramble. There was no telling how far I'd go or what I'd see. North Carolina was just the first step.

I must have dozed off again because the next thing I knew June was shouting in my ear, "We're almost there, we're almost there. The conductor said Grandville's the next stop!"

I shifted Victor from my lap to the floor, steadying him with my legs. Darned if he hadn't wet his pants and mine, too.

While I was wondering what I was going to do about it, June squeezed my arm. "Gordy, do you suppose they named Grandville after Grandma?"

"What are you talking about? Her name's Aitcheson, not Grand."

"Her name's *Grandma*," June said, scowling at me. "And the town is called *Grand*ville."

I started to laugh, but then I remembered how easy it was to hurt June's feelings. Across the aisle, Bobby was already crying and Ernie was tuning up. Victor was whining his stomach hurt. I didn't want to get off the train with everybody bawling but Mama and me.

"Maybe you're right, Junie," I said. "That would make Grandma a real important person, wouldn't it?"

June nodded and smoothed her dress. "Do I look pretty?"

"Sure you do," I lied. The truth was, her hair was ratty with tangles, her dress was stained with the apple juice she'd spilled at breakfast, and she had that pale, sickly look she gets when she's tired.

"That's good," she said. "I want Grandma to think I'm a pretty little girl. I want her to love me."

To my relief, I didn't have to say anything because the conductor came down the aisle, bellowing, "Grandville, everybody off for Grandville."

By the time the train stopped, we were standing at the door, ready for our first look at Grandma and Grandville both. I hoped she and the town were ready for us.

Three

❖ ❖ ❖ ❖ ❖ ❖ ❖ ❖

I guess I'd expected Grandma to be a beaten-down old woman, poor and shabby like us, but the tall white-haired lady walking toward us looked like a queen.

Junie tugged at my jacket. "I told you she was grand, didn't I? Didn't I, Gordy?"

I nodded, holding my bag of clothes so it hid the wet spot Victor had left on my pants. Not that anyone was paying a speck of attention to us kids. Grandma and Mama stood face to face, staring at each other. I swear they looked like enemies meeting on a battlefield. No hugs, no kisses, no smiles, no glad words. Just eyeball-to-eyeball silence.

Mama was the first to look away, but Grandma was the first to speak. "For pity's sake, stand up straight, Virginia," she said, "and get that hangdog look off your face."

Mama didn't raise her head. She ran one hand

through her hair and kept on staring at the station plat-
form. Not one word did she say.

Ernie and Bobby more than made up for Mama's
silence by bawling like calves. Victor just stood there,
picking his nose as if he didn't have all his buttons.
When I slapped his hand, he called me a name I knew
Grandma wouldn't like. Then he hauled off and kicked
me.

While I tried to make Victor behave, I glanced at
June. She was standing up straight and tall, waiting for
Grandma to notice her and smiling so hard it hurt to
look at her. If you ever saw a puppy at the pound,
that's what June reminded me of. Pale and dirty and
skinny but hopeful. If she'd had a tail, she'd have been
wagging it to beat the band.

Mama pulled us forward one at a time and intro-
duced us. It seemed to me Grandma was more shocked
than happy to meet all us kids. Mama hadn't seen her
or talked to her for years, not since she'd eloped with
the old man and scandalized the whole town. Now
she'd come home. Maybe she hadn't said exactly how
many kids she was bringing with her.

"And this is Gordy," Mama said, nudging me forward.

Before Grandma said anything, she looked behind
me as if she feared there might be a few more grandchildren back there. Then she shook my hand and said
she was glad to meet me, which was what she'd said to
everybody else.

Without another word she led us to an old black
Packard, about the biggest car I'd ever seen. "There's

plenty of room for you all," she said, and settled herself behind the steering wheel. Mama got in beside her, still toting Bobby, whose odor hadn't improved. I saw Grandma twitch her nose, but she didn't say anything.

The rest of us piled into the back. June was still smiling but I was sure her face was starting to ache from the effort.

If Mama and Grandma spoke to each other I couldn't hear what they said for the noise of whining and bawling and fussing coming from my brothers, combined with the sound of the car's engine. I was about deafened by the racket.

A few minutes later, Grandma pulled into a long driveway and parked beside a house so big it just about took my breath away. There wasn't a place in College Hill to match it. Not even up on the hill where the richest families lived. I figured we'd stopped here to pick something up. No kin of ours lived in a mansion like this.

But I was wrong. Mama got out of the car and started walking toward the house. It was clear she knew exactly where she was going.

June looked at me. "Is Grandma a millionaire, Gordy?"

"How do I know?" I guess I sounded cross, but it seemed to me Mama should have told me what to expect. With Stuart and Donny gone, I was the oldest son. Surely I had a right to be informed.

June's eyes filled with tears. "You don't have to get mad, Gordy. I just asked you a question, that's all."

I patted her head and said I was sorry. By the time Grandma led us into a big cool hallway, June was smiling again. But the person she was trying so hard to impress didn't even look her way.

"Come along," Grandma said, snapping her fingers as if we were trained dogs about to jump through hoops.

Upstairs, Grandma began assigning bedrooms and telling us where the bathroom was and things like that. I'd never heard such a bossy woman. She was even worse than my old teacher Mrs. Wagner.

June and I got our own private rooms, something we'd never had before. My three brothers all went into a room next to Mama's. The biggest bedroom running across the back of the house was Grandma's. I figured out Grandpa was dead though nobody actually said so.

"Wash up," Grandma said. "Dinner will be ready at five thirty sharp."

We all stood in the hall and watched her go downstairs. *Click click* went her shoes, firm and quick on each step. Then she was gone.

I turned to Mama. She was staring into the emptiness Grandma had left behind. Her face had the same old blank look it always had. "Why didn't you tell me she was rich?" I asked.

Mama didn't look at me. "It's not important."

"Not important?" I stared at Mama in disbelief. "What do you mean? All those times the old man was out of work, you could have called Grandma, you could have brought us down here, you could have left him."

My voice was shooting up like a girl's, getting shrill and whiny, but Mama just stood there, round-shouldered and sad, staring at the empty hall. Without saying a word, she picked up Bobby and headed for the bathroom. Victor and Ernie followed her, leaving June and me alone at the top of the stairs.

"Do you think she's glad we're here, Gordy?" June asked.

"Grandma? Darned if I know, Junie. She hasn't said much one way or the other."

"Did you see how I was smiling and looking pretty?"

"Sure."

"I don't think Grandma noticed," June said sadly.

"She had other stuff on her mind. What to give us for dinner and all." I paused and took a good look at my sister. "When Mama's done in the bathroom, wash your hands and face and comb your hair. Get Mama to braid it for you. Change your dress, too."

June looked mournful. "Mama will be too tired to braid my hair," she said. "And my other dress has the hem ripped out. It's too small, too."

I hung my head and stared at the shadows slanting across the steps. There was nothing I could do to help June. I couldn't mend her dress or braid her hair. Besides, I was a mess myself. My pants were still damp and they smelled like Victor's pee. My shirt was missing two buttons and both my shoestrings were broken. Maybe Mama had belonged in this house once, but the whole bunch of us seemed out of place now, her included.

Kicking at the corner of a fancy little rug, I sighed. As usual, nothing was going right. We might as well have stayed in our old house on Davis Road. If I'd been Victor's age, I'd have cried. But I was the oldest now. I had to be tough for everybody.

Four

❖   ❖   ❖   ❖   ❖   ❖   ❖   ❖

At about five thirty, Grandma called us to dinner. It smelled so good I just about broke my neck running downstairs to see what it was. The sight of the food made my stomach come to attention with a growl so loud June giggled. Grandma had gone all out. Fried chicken, mashed potatoes drowning in gravy, biscuits piled high, fresh tomatoes, and some homemade relishes. I hadn't seen a meal like that since way back before the war. And maybe not even then.

But, much as I liked the food, I can't say I enjoyed eating it. In fact, if I hadn't been so hungry, I would have gone back to my room. Grandma was after us about our manners from the minute we sat down. She fussed at June for having her elbows on the table. Victor and Ernie horrified her by chewing with their mouths open. Bobby ate with his fingers. I didn't hold my fork, spoon, or knife right. Nor did I say please when I asked Mama to pass me the butter. I also ate too fast. And hunched over my plate as though I expected someone to steal my dinner, as Grandma put it.

"You haven't taught these children a thing, Virginia," Grandma said, sounding just as snooty as mean old Mrs. Wagner. "They behave as if they'd been brought up in a barn. It's positively disgraceful."

Mama stared silently at her plate, but she didn't say a thing. I glared at her, vexed by the way she just sat there. Why didn't she speak up?

"Maybe we like barns," I said, figuring it was up to me to defend us. "Maybe we like being disgraceful."

"You watch your tongue, young man," Grandma said.

At the same moment, June spilled her milk. At the sight of it spreading across the tablecloth, she began to cry.

Turning to her, Grandma said, "Hush. If there's one thing I cannot abide, it's crying."

"I'm trying so hard to be good," June wailed. "Can't you see how hard I'm trying?"

"Don't talk back" was what Grandma said to that. Grabbing a napkin, she began sopping up the milk.

By now I was beginning to see why Mama had run away with the old man. Too bad he turned out to be even worse than Grandma.

After dinner, Grandma told Mama to put the little kids to bed. "I'm going into the living room to listen to the war news," she said to June and me. "You're welcome to come with me, but you must be quiet. I won't tolerate talking while the news is on."

Behind Grandma's back, I Heil-Hitlered her and then goose-stepped into the living room. That made June giggle, but it didn't make me feel any better about things.

June and I sat down near the radio and Grandma made herself comfortable in an armchair. Gabriel Heatter had good news for us. On the Eastern Front, the Russians were across the Oder, fighting the Nazis in Breslau. On the Western Front, we were crossing the Ruhr, heading straight into what Heatter called Germany's industrial heartland. Things were getting better on Iwo Jima and we were bombing the Japs in Manila. Grandma actually smiled.

When the news was over, she let June listen to "Fibber McGee and Molly," her favorite comedy show. But Grandma had some questions for me.

"You have two brothers in the army," she said. "Donald is somewhere in Europe, I believe."

"Donny's in Germany," I said, eager to brag. "Though he's not supposed to say, I figure he's in Patton's Third Army. You know, with Old Blood and Guts, chasing Krauts across France and into Germany. He was in the Battle of the Bulge, too. I bet he comes home with every medal you can get. Maybe even the Congressional Medal of Honor—"

Grandma cut me off with the question I'd been trying to keep her from asking. "And Stuart? What about him?"

"Stu? Uh, he's in a military hospital," I said, starting with the truth. But I finished with a lie. "He was wounded in Italy or someplace. They shipped him back here."

Grandma gazed at me, her eyes narrowed. "Is that right?"

"No, Gordy," June piped up. "Don't you remember? Stu stayed in the woods. You hid him in your hut so he wouldn't have to go to the war. He's in the hospital 'cause Daddy hit him."

"That's what your mother told me." Grandma eyed me coldly. "You might as well admit it, Gordon. Stuart deserted."

"What if he did?" I asked. "It doesn't make him yellow or anything. He thinks war's wrong, that's all." My face was so hot I thought my head might explode. I'd been taking up for my brother long enough. I was sick of it—sick of him and Grandma, too. Old bat, asking me questions she already knew the answer to.

"I'm not like Stu," I yelled. "I'd fight if I was old enough. In fact I hope the war lasts till I'm eighteen so I can go kill Nazis like Donny!"

"If you don't learn to control that temper," Grandma said, "you'll follow in your father's footsteps, Gordon Smith."

I jumped to my feet. "I'll never be like that SOB!"

"That's enough impudence for one night," Grandma said. "Go to bed right now!"

I gave June a dirty look but she was staring at the radio as if she expected to see Fibber McGee step out onto the living room carpet. "Don't open the closet," she chanted, "don't open the closet!"

But of course Fibber did, and everything fell out with a big crash like always, and his wife Molly got mad like always. June laughed and so did all the people in the studio audience.

"You heard me, Gordon," Grandma said, pointing at the stairs as if she was banishing a dog who'd peed on the carpet. "Go to bed. Now."

"Don't worry," I sneered. "I wouldn't stay here if you paid me." Without looking at Grandma or June, I swaggered out of the room. A loud burst of laughter from the radio spoiled my exit somewhat but I kept on going.

Not long after I got into bed, I heard June come upstairs. She paused at my door. I figured she wanted to apologize for starting the trouble between Grandma and me, but instead of knocking she just stood there a few moments and then went on to her room. Maybe she thought I was asleep.

A little later, a train went by. Though it wasn't close enough to shake the bed the way it did back home, I could hear the whistle and the sound of the engine. Lord, I wished I was on it, heading for the Gulf Stream waters and the redwood forest and the sparkling sands of the diamond deserts. Instead I was stuck here in Grandville, North Carolina, in a big old mansion with the coldest-hearted grandma who ever drew breath.

When the train was gone, the night seemed lonelier. Quieter, too. The floor creaked, the stairs squeaked, I thought I heard June whimpering in her sleep. The wind blew through the big old tree outside, shaking the bare branches. Not far away, a dog barked.

I was just starting to fall asleep when voices outside my door woke me up. Angry voices. Not loud but deadly low, which was worse somehow.

"You're almost forty years old, Virginia," Grandma was saying, "and you come crawling home like a whipped dog. Where is your pride? Your dignity? Your spirit? Did you let that man beat every ounce of gumption out of you?"

"If you don't want us, say so," Mama whispered. "We'll leave, Mother."

"Where would you go with those pitiful children?"

Pitiful children—is that how Grandma saw us? I had half a mind to go out there and tell the old battle-axe a thing or two. Let her say Gordy Smith was pitiful then.

"I don't know where I'd go." Mama's voice sank even lower. "That's why I came here, I thought maybe you would . . . that is, I hoped . . . I mean . . ."

Grandma said nothing.

"This was my home once," Mama said, speaking a little louder.

"You were certainly anxious to leave it when you were sixteen," Grandma said. "It was Roger you wanted then, not your father or me."

"Mother, what do you want me to say? I made a mistake, I was wrong, I'm sorry!" Mama's voice rose. It was all I could do not to cheer her on.

Trouble was, she woke up Bobby. He started crying, which roused Ernie and Victor.

"You made your bed," Grandma said. "Now sleep in

it—if you can find room." A few seconds later, her door slammed shut.

Mama must have gone to my brothers' room because I soon heard her singing to them, trying to lull them back to sleep with sad war songs.

The moment the house got quiet, June tiptoed into my room, sniffling, and perched on the edge of my bed. It seemed I was never going to get any sleep, so I sat up and asked her what was wrong.

"It's just like home," she sobbed, "only now it's Mama and Grandma fighting instead of her and Daddy. Why can't everybody be nice to each other?"

"At least Grandma didn't hit Mama," I said. "Or us."

"She says mean things, though," June said.

I patted her shoulder. "You know what they say, June Bug. 'Sticks and stones may break my bones—'"

"'But harsh words cannot hurt me,'" June finished in a singsong voice. Sticking her thumb in her mouth, she crawled into bed beside me. "Can I sleep here just for tonight?"

"If you promise not to kick me black and blue."

"I'll lie way over here beside the wall," June promised, "and I won't move all night long."

June fell asleep almost at once, but I lay awake for hours, listening to trains thunder past, blowing their whistles to warn folks they were coming. I was out of College Hill but I wasn't sure I was in a better place. Like June said, it was the same old thing as before, fighting and arguing and people crying. But at least the old man wasn't here. That had to be an improvement.

Five

❖ ❖ ❖ ❖ ❖ ❖ ❖ ❖ ❖

The next day was Saturday. The first thing Grandma did was organize a shopping trip. She said she wasn't about to have a raggedy bunch of poor white trash grandchildren living in her house. After she made sure we were all scrubbed clean, she loaded us into her big old Packard and drove us downtown. First stop was the barber shop for everybody but Mama and June. Then we went to Goode's Department Store, where we all got outfitted with everything from socks and underwear to church clothes.

Everybody but Mama, that is. Even though Grandma offered, Mama said she didn't want anything.

"But, Mama," June pleaded, "you need a new dress. Think how pretty you'd look in one like that."

Mama glanced at the dress June was pointing at and shook her head. "Don't be silly," she said.

At home, Grandma sent us upstairs to put on our

new playclothes, as she called them. When we came down, she lined us up from youngest to oldest and studied us, tidying Victor's hair, tying Bobby's shoelaces, straightening June's part, tucking Ernie's jersey into his overalls. "Well," she said at last, "you look presentable. Now let's see if you can act presentable."

After lunch, all the kids followed me into the backyard. To get away from them, I climbed the big oak tree beside the garage. Luckily they wandered off to play on an old-fashioned wooden swing set, leaving me free to scramble from branch to branch like Tarzan till I was as high as I wanted to be, which was pretty high. I surveyed the whole neighborhood. All the houses were big. Some had towers like Grandma's, others were plainer, but none was shabby or run-down. The paint on all of them was fresh, the grass in the big yards as green as it's likely to be in February, the bushes neatly trimmed. No trash anywhere. Nothing broken-down or ramshackle.

Shrieks of laughter drew my attention to June and Victor. They were pumping the swing, making it go as high as possible, while Ernie ran around it, wailing, "Me, too! Me, too!" Bobby stood a few feet away, a thumb in his mouth, watching. I thought I saw Mama's face at the kitchen window but it might have been the reflection of a cloud.

From high over their heads, I studied my sister and brothers, trying to decide if they still looked like Smiths. To a stranger, they might seem to be ordinary, everyday kids, but, in spite of their new clothes, there was something about them, a Smith-ness you couldn't quite wash off. Maybe it was that puppy-in-the-pound smile June gave everybody or the way Bobby sucked his thumb or the sad look in Victor's eyes. Misfits, that's what they looked like. Mama and the old man, Stu and Donny and me—none of us really fit in anywhere.

A door opened in the house next door, and a pale, thin woman came outside carrying a basket of laundry. She was younger than Mama and pretty in a kind of nervous way. A widow, I thought, remembering the gold star I'd seen in her front window. Back in College Hill, lots of folks had stars to show they'd lost somebody in the war. I'd known a few of the ones who got killed, guys who'd been my brothers' buddies. It was tough to think they'd never come back and play ball on the field by the train tracks. One had been good enough to pitch for the Senators.

The woman next door took her time hanging out the clothes, mainly because she was giving most of her attention to my sister and brothers, who were still whooping it up on the swing set. No more nosy than the average snoop, she'd probably heard we were coming and wanted to get a good look at us. She didn't see me spying on her from the tree.

What interested me most were the shirts, jerseys, and trousers she was hanging up. Those clothes meant she had a son. He was smaller than I was—I could tell by the size of his clothes—but big enough to pal around with. Maybe he and I could start a gang like I had in College Hill, get in a little trouble, do things to make life interesting.

After the woman went back inside, I sat in the tree and stared at the shut door, wishing the boy would come out. It was a nice day, not too cold but a little windy, perfect weather for fooling around.

Suddenly the curtain twitched at an upstairs window just about level with the branch I was sitting on. For a second, I glimpsed a pale face looking at me, but it disappeared before I could grin or wave or do anything.

At the same moment Grandma spotted me. "Gordon Smith," she called from the back door. "Come down from that tree before you break your neck."

I took my time in case the boy next door was watching. It wouldn't do for him to think I was some goody-goody kid.

Before I followed Grandma inside, I took a long look at the second-floor window of the house next door. The curtain twitched again, I swear it did, and I got the funniest feeling I was being watched. Why didn't the boy open the window and show his face? Say something friendly? Either he was a stuck-up snob or he didn't have all his marbles, spying on me like that.

To let him know what I thought of sneaks, I gave the boy the finger real quick so Grandma wouldn't see. He probably wasn't anybody I wanted to be friends with, so I figured I'd beat him up when I saw him. He couldn't hide in his house forever.

Six

❖ ❖ ❖ ❖ ❖ ❖ ❖ ❖ ❖

At dinner I asked Grandma who lived next door. "Mrs. Sullivan and her son, William," she said. Turning to Mama, she added, "You might remember Shirley. She's Lorna Tuttle's youngest sister." She paused to sip her tea, watching Mama all the time. "She married Bill Sullivan who died in the war. Shot down on a mission over Holland, I think."

Without looking up from her plate, Mama said, "I vaguely remember Lorna, but I don't recall Shirley at all."

"She's a nice young woman," Grandma went on. "Losing Bill was a terrible blow to her. It's been two years and she hasn't gotten over it yet."

Grandma went on talking about people Mama had known, telling her what had happened to them in the years she'd been gone. Some were fighting overseas, some had died in the war. Others had left town like Mama. A few had stayed in Grandville. They had families and jobs.

Once in a while, Mama nodded or said, "Is that right?" But it was clear she wasn't really interested in any of them. Finally Grandma gave up. Which gave me a chance to ask about William.

"How come he didn't come outside to meet me?" I asked. "He was spying on me from his window. I saw the curtains move."

Grandma finished chewing a mouthful of Spam and washed it down with a swallow of tea. All the while, she seemed to be thinking of how to answer my question. At last she said, "William's an invalid, Gordon."

"What's wrong with him?" I asked, surprised by Grandma's answer. Here I'd been thinking the kid was a snob, and he was sick—which seemed to rule out being friends *or* enemies with him.

Grandma regarded me steadily as if she was trying to figure out what I was thinking. "He had a bad case of polio last summer," she said.

June drew in her breath. Her eyes widened. "Is he in an iron lung?"

Like June, I stared at Grandma, my dinner forgotten. If there was one thing I was scared of, it was polio. A boy I knew had died of it in College Hill. He went to bed feeling fine and woke up in the middle of the night, saying his head hurt. His folks took him to the hospital, and two days later he died. He was only six years old, poor kid.

Iron lungs were almost as scary as dying. I'd seen a picture of one in *Life* magazine. This woman's head stuck out of a long tube. The rest of her was inside, paralyzed. She couldn't even breathe by herself, but she'd learned to write and draw holding a pencil between her teeth. To stay alive, she had to lie in that thing day and night.

"The poor child can breathe just fine," Grandma told June. "But his legs are so weak he can't walk."

"Like President Roosevelt," June said solemnly.

Grandma nodded, her face serious. Judging by the picture of Roosevelt hanging over the living room radio, I figured she liked the president a lot more than the old man did. He blamed everything in the world on FDR, including the war and the Depression before that, things everyone knew weren't Roosevelt's fault. To listen to the old man, you'd think the New Deal was responsible for all our troubles.

Fit to bust with curiosity, I leaned toward Grandma, eager to learn more about William. "Where did he get polio?" I asked. "The swimming pool? The movies? A carnival?"

"No one knows for sure," Grandma said, "but his mother suspects he caught it playing in the creek that runs under the train tracks just outside town."

I made a silent promise to stay away from that creek, just in case. "Does he wear braces on his legs? Can he walk with crutches or does he have a wheelchair?"

"You ask too many questions, Gordon." Grandma looked around the table. "Finish your dinner, children. There's apple pie for those who clean their plates."

"Can I go see William?" I asked.

Grandma shook her head. "Wait until Shirley invites you. William's delicate. He mustn't be exposed to germs. With him, an ordinary cold can turn to pneumonia overnight."

"I'm healthy," I said. "I don't have any contagious diseases or germs or anything."

Grandma shook her head. No dice. It was up to Mrs. Sullivan. If she invited me, I could go.

The conversation, such as it was, drifted aimlessly. No matter what Grandma talked about, Mama made no answer. She just sat there fidgeting with her napkin ring, looking as glum as ever. Maybe she'd been unhappy so long she'd forgotten how to be happy.

Finally Grandma asked Mama the question I'd been dreading. "What about school, Virginia? Gordon and June have to be enrolled. Maybe Victor should be in kindergarten."

Mama shrugged and went on toying with the napkin ring. "What's the sense of putting them in school?"

"It's the law, Virginia." Grandma spoke as if Mama was no older than June. "Children must go to school. Do you want the truant officer to come calling on us?"

Mama shrugged again. "If it's so important, take Gordy and June over there on Monday, but leave Victor here. He won't turn five till September."

I ate my pie but my pleasure in it was gone. School—I might have known Grandma would think of it.

That's how I came to be in Miss Whipple's sixth

grade class at Grandville Elementary School. Compared to Old Lady Wagner, my teacher in College Hill, she wasn't too bad. At least she didn't keep hankies down the front of her dress or recite long boring poems about village smithies under spreading chestnut trees. But she believed in fractions and decimals the way preachers believe in Jesus. From the minute she laid eyes on me, she did her best to convert me to the holy religion of math.

"Do you know how to change fractions to decimals, Gordon?" she asked.

I could tell the other kids were looking at me, sizing me up, wondering if I was some smart-aleck Yankee kid come down here to show off. I slouched in my desk, sticking my feet way out in the aisle, and smirked. "Do I look like Einstein?"

A few kids snickered but Miss Whipple merely shook her head. "No," she said, "you most definitely do not resemble Einstein." Pausing a moment, she added, "After school, I'll give you some tests. They should tell me what you know and what you don't know."

"That shouldn't take long," a boy behind me muttered just loud enough for me to hear. "Most likely he doesn't know anything."

I turned around to give him a dirty look but he didn't seem the least bit scared of me. He just sat there like he was daring me to say something.

At recess the boy walked up to me, followed by two or three of his toadies. By now I knew who he was—Jerry Langerman, the Gordy Smith of Grandville.

"So you're from Maryland," he said, stepping so close to me I could smell his chewing gum. Doublemint, I guessed.

"That's a Union state," he went on, shoving his face at me. "Which means your great-granddaddy fought against my great-granddaddy. Maybe even killed him." He shoved me hard. "Damn Yankee."

I knew it would do no good to tell Langerman my mother was from Grandville and had Rebel kin. So I let him think what he wanted. Besides, it gave me an excuse to shove him back. Nobody pushed Gordy Smith around. Not even guys half a foot taller than me and a lot heavier.

"Damn Rebel," I yelled, pushing him so hard he staggered.

Langerman swore and lunged at me, punching me hard in the stomach. From then on it was his fists and mine with no time for name-calling.

Just as I was getting the better of him, some kid ran for the teacher. In no time, Langerman and I found ourselves in the principal's office.

"What brings you in here, Jerry?" Mr. Malone asked. Something in the man's look and voice warned me he wasn't on my side. Which didn't surprise me.

"This little Yankee cussed the South, sir," Jerry said, "and then he took a swing at me. It was my duty to defend myself—and the honor of North Carolina."

Mr. Malone's small eyes turned to me. He had a round red face and a big neck that spread over his shirt collar like cherry Jell-O. "We don't tolerate profanity at this school, or fighting, boy," he said. "You owe Jerry an apology."

"I don't owe him anything," I said, narrowing my eyes to mean little slits to show everybody I wasn't scared of any dumb principal.

Mr. Malone's fat fingers curled around a ruler. Heaving himself to his feet, he said, "Hold out your hands, boy. You're in for some corporal punishment. If you don't know the meaning of the term, I'll teach it to you fast."

While Jerry stood there grinning, the principal whacked my hands till they stung so hard I thought they'd fall off. I didn't say a word, though. I'd lived through a lot worse than being hit with a skinny old ruler.

"Let that be a lesson to you," Mr. Malone said. "The next time I catch you fighting, I'll use the paddle on you."

I walked out of the office without looking back. Behind me, I heard the principal say, "Be sure and tell your daddy those pills he prescribed are helping, Jerry. He's a damn fine doctor, boy, damn fine."

When Jerry caught up with me, I said, "Just wait. I'll fix you and your great-granddaddy, too."

The look on his face was worth the rabbit punch he gave me.

At home, I got in trouble all over again. For one thing, my brand-new jersey was ripped at the neck.

For another, I had a swollen lip. Worst of all, the principal had called Grandma and told her the details of my first day in Grandville Elementary School.

"Fighting like a common hooligan," she said. "Staying after school, failing tests, smirking when Miss Whipple corrected you. This won't do, Gordon."

I shrugged. "I hate school."

"Why?"

I stared at Grandma, surprised. Nobody had ever asked me why I hated school. "I'm dumb."

"I don't believe that," Grandma said.

June looked up from the picture she was drawing at the kitchen table. "It's true," she said, trying to be helpful, I guess. "Gordy's always been dumb. He almost fails every single grade."

"The only reason they pass me is because no teacher wants me two years in a row," I boasted.

Grandma made a little sniffing noise. "That I can believe."

"Look, Grandma, see my picture?" June shoved her drawing toward Grandma. "It's you and me in the house looking out the windows. I drew one just like it for my teacher and she said it was good. Do you like it?"

Grandma's mouth twitched the teeniest bit. If it had been someone else, I'd have said it was a smile, but on her it was hard to tell.

"You've made the heads too big," Grandma said. "They'd never fit inside that little house."

June snatched her drawing back. The smiling sun,

the happy faces, and the big bird flying past disappeared as she wadded the picture into a ball.

"Now what did you go and do that for?" Grandma asked. "You wasted a perfectly good piece of paper. You could have drawn something else on the back."

June kept her head down but I could see she was trying not to cry. "It was a good picture," I said, but my sister didn't care what I thought.

Grandma reached out real slow and touched June's hand so briefly I doubt my sister even noticed. "There's nothing wrong with a little constructive criticism," she said in a let's-make-up voice. "It was nice the way you drew the sun with a big grin on its face. And the bird was good, too. It's just that the house was too small for you and me to fit in without bumping our heads on the ceiling."

Instead of answering, June threw the wad of paper into the trash can. She left the kitchen, letting the screen door slam behind her.

For once, Grandma didn't scold her. Turning to me, she said crossly, "You've got homework, Gordon. I want to see you do it."

I'd had enough. "You're not my mother," I said, and followed June outside. I let the screen door slam too.

I heard Grandma yelling for me to come back and finish my homework, but I climbed up into the tree and sat there till dinnertime. Nobody told Gordy Smith what to do—not the old man, not Miss Whipple, not the principal, not Grandma.

I went to bed that night without dinner. That's what

I got for talking back to Grandma. Even though my stomach growled so loud it kept me awake, I was glad I'd stuck up for myself. Never had I done a lick of homework, and I didn't intend to start now. Suppose word got back to College Hill. What would my old friends and enemies think of me?

Seven

❖ ❖ ❖ ❖ ❖ ❖ ❖ ❖

Somehow I got through my first week in Grandville. At school I played dumb the way I always had. I did nothing all day but draw fighter planes, tanks, destroyers, and soldiers shooting each other. If Miss Whipple called on me, I pretended not to know the answer. I messed up my math problems on purpose. I misspelled every word on my spelling test. I wrote my vocabulary sentences without periods or commas, running the words together so they made no sense. Soon Miss Whipple gave up on me and let me sit there drawing planes and tanks and soldiers.

After a week of school, I was ready for Saturday. But not for rain. It wasn't just a sprinkle but a hard all-day downpour that never let up and kept us all inside till we felt like the people in June's picture—too big for Grandma's house.

Sunday the rain stopped but we couldn't go outside because, as soon as we got back from church, Grandma was expecting company. Relatives. Not a single Smith, just Aitchesons. I asked her why that was.

"Didn't the old man come from Grandville too? Doesn't he have some relatives here?" It wasn't that I had a yen to see his kin. I just wanted to know about them. Be prepared in case they were as bad as he was. Or even worse.

Grandma shook her head. "Your father was in the navy when he met your mother. If he has any family, I don't know their whereabouts."

That was a relief.

Grandma made sure we all looked as nice as possible. We were to be on our best behavior, too. "Old folks are coming that haven't seen your mother since she eloped with your father. I expect you to be polite."

Maybe it was my imagination, but it seemed to me Grandma aimed most of her warnings at yours truly.

I glanced at Mama once or twice while Grandma combed my brothers' hair and tucked in their shirts and retied their shoes. She didn't appear to be interested in helping or anything else. Hadn't done her hair or put on lipstick. Her dress was split under one arm.

While Grandma bustled around, Mama sat in an armchair and gazed at the radio as if she was listening to it, but I doubt she could have told you what song was playing. Ever since we'd come to Grandville, she'd taken less and less notice of things, us included. What was going on inside her head was anybody's guess, but it worried me to see her looking so dull and vacant. I'd thought once we got away from the old man, she'd perk up, but it seemed I was dead wrong.

When the doorbell chimed, June followed Grandma to the door. She had that puppy-in-the-pound smile glued to her face. You'd think she was hoping to be adopted.

For the next half hour, people poured into the house. Great-uncles and great-aunts and a few cousins once or twice removed. Twelve altogether and not one under sixty. I never saw so many canes. It's a wonder they didn't trip each other.

June fluttered among them, smiling and dimpling like Shirley Temple. I wouldn't have been surprised if she'd started to sing "The Good Ship Lollipop" or some other cornball song. Maybe tap-danced, too.

Sappy or not, June charmed the whole room— which was more than the rest of us did. Bobby pooped in his pants and had to be whisked away by Grandma. Ernie sucked his thumb and Victor picked his nose. They refused to shake Great-uncle Henry's hand. They refused to sit on Great-aunt Mabel's lap. They got into the chocolate cake when nobody was looking and smeared it all over themselves and the carpet.

Mama sat in her chair and tried to be invisible. She never spoke unless she was spoken to and then said only what was required, which was usually, "I'm just fine, thank you."

I sneaked out to the kitchen every chance I got, but Grandma kept coming after me and sending me back to the living room. Warning me to behave. Reminding me

I was the oldest, it was my job to set an example for Victor and Ernie.

So I shook hands with Great-uncle Henry and told everyone who asked how old I was and what my favorite school subject was—they thought I was kidding when I said "Recess."

I was doing pretty good until Great-aunt Mavis came along. She was the worst of the bunch, a skinny old lady with a long pointed nose who scared June because she looked exactly like the witch in her *Snow White* book.

I'd been avoiding Great-aunt Mavis for fear she'd grab hold of me and kiss me the way she'd kissed the other kids. But I happened to be nearby when she decided to engage Mama in conversation.

"Why, Virginia, I almost didn't recognize you," she said in a phony sweet voice just gushing with concern and sympathy. "Bless your little heart, you used to be the prettiest girl in Grandville, honey."

That's when I lost my temper. While Mama stared at the floor, all mousy and sad, I looked Great-aunt Mavis in the eye and said, "At least Mama was pretty once. I bet that's more than anyone ever said of you!"

Mama gazed at me as if she didn't entirely grasp the full extent of my rudeness, but Great-aunt Mavis just about turned purple. The glass plate she was holding tipped and all her little macaroons slid into her lap.

"How dare you—" she began, but I was already halfway out the door, running as if I planned to make it back to College Hill in time for supper.

Eight

❖ ❖ ❖ ❖ ❖ ❖ ❖ ❖ ❖

The last thing I heard before the door slammed shut was Great-aunt Mavis saying, "That boy has some ugly ways."

"My ugly ways against your ugly face," I yelled as I ran down the porch steps. Even though the old witch couldn't have heard me, I felt better for saying it.

As I headed for the street, I glanced at the Sullivans' house. Once more I saw the curtains twitching at the same window on the second floor. "Get a camera," I hollered, "you nosy little twerp."

I'd gotten as far as the school when I saw Jerry Langerman. He and his buddy, Joe Ellinghaus, were fooling around on the playground, shooting baskets and showing off their pitiful vocabulary of cuss words.

When Langerman spotted me, he sauntered across the asphalt, bouncing the basketball. Ellinghaus tagged along with him like a shadow at noon, short and dense.

"Well, well," Langerman drawled, "look who's here. The damn Yankee himself, all dressed up for his own funeral."

I'd clean forgotten I was wearing my best clothes and no doubt looked like a dumb old sissy. Which couldn't have been further from the truth. Stepping closer, I eyeballed Langerman, but before I could hit him, he said, "How's your old man like being in jail?"

It seemed Grandville was getting more like College Hill every day. There was just no end to gossip and small-town nastiness. "Ask your old man," I said. "I bet he's been there once or twice."

"That's a laugh," Ellinghaus said. "Jerry's father is Dr. Langerman."

He said this as if I should fall down dead with awe or something, but I already knew about Langerman's daddy and the pills he gave the principal. "So what?"

"So this." Langerman yanked my tie, and Ellinghaus hee-hawed like the jackass he was.

I shoved Langerman hard enough to make him drop the basketball. "Why don't you get your ugly face out of here?" I sneered. "The sight of you is enough to kill a person. And the stink's even worse."

Langerman shoved me back. "Shut your Yankee trap, Smith, or I'll shut it for you."

"You and who else?"

Langerman lunged at me, hitting, kicking, using every low method of fighting he knew, including pulling my hair and trying to choke me with the stupid tie I was wearing. I happened to know a few tricks myself, and by the time we were done with each other, both our noses were bleeding. His lip was cut, and I had a black eye. Our shirts were ripped, too. We were still cussing each other, but I was way ahead of him in the use of bad language. My brother Donny had taught me a lot, and so had the old man. I doubt fancy-pants Langerman knew anyone like the pair of them.

Finally he and Ellinghaus went one way, still yelling insults, and I turned to go the other, yelling just as loud. It looked like I wasn't going to make any friends in Grandville. Which didn't surprise me.

At the corner I shouted one last insult at Langerman and then headed for home. That's when I saw William for the first time. He was sitting in a wheelchair on his front porch. A plaid blanket covered his legs. His face was as thin and white as an old man's, and his hands were skinny claws. A fringe of dark hair hid his forehead but not his eyes, which were big and gray and fixed on me as if he'd never seen my like before.

"What are *you* looking at?" I asked.

"Nothing." William started to roll his chair toward the door.

"Wait a minute," I said.

He turned and looked at me.

"How come you always spy on me?" I asked.

"I don't," he said.

"Yes, you do. I see your window curtains twitch whenever I'm fooling around in Grandma's yard."

"I suppose I can look out my own window if I feel like it. So far as I know, there's no law against that."

For a cripple he was pretty uppity, I thought. "If you're so smart, why aren't you in school?"

William gave me a look meant to cut me dead and started rolling himself toward the door again.

I rattled off a few cuss words and called him a name that would get most kids' mouths washed out with laundry soap. It was the only way to defend myself. I couldn't hit him or anything, that was clear.

It was just my luck that the door opened before I was finished and there was William's mother, staring at me as if I were the devil himself.

"William," she said, "is that boy bothering you?"

"Him?" William loaded his voice with scorn. "He's a moron. He couldn't bother me if he tried."

With that he went inside and the door slammed behind him. But not before his mother gave me a look that plainly said I hadn't heard the last of this.

Since the relatives' cars were still parked in the driveway, I climbed up the tree and sat on a branch, waiting for them to leave. Pretty soon the window curtain twitched and I knew William was watching me again. I made my worst face and gave him the finger again, but I knew he was still there, snickering at me no doubt, thinking I was a moron.

After a while June came outside and spotted me in the tree. She tried to climb up but was too short to reach the lowest branches, so she had to stay on the ground. "Where've you been, Gordy? You're all dirty. Did you get in a fight?"

"What if I did?"

June shrugged and twirled a curl around her finger. "Everybody's mad at you," she said.

"So what else is new?"

"Grandma's going to make you 'pologize to Great-aunt Mavis."

"There's not a snowball's chance in hell of me doing that."

June pressed her hands over her mouth. "Gordy, you said a bad word."

"I could say a whole lot worse if I wanted to."

"You better not." June walked around the tree a couple of times, singing something about a mulberry bush.

I wished she'd go back to the house and leave me be, but she stopped and looked up at me again. "The lady next door called Grandma and said you were rude to her little boy. You'll probably have to 'pologize to him, too."

This time I just snorted. Grandma had a lot to learn about me. She could lock me in a closet, she could feed me bread and water, she could beat me black and blue, but I wouldn't apologize to anyone. Gordy Smith never said he was sorry. If Grandma didn't believe me, she could ask the principal.

"Aren't you cold?" June asked after a while.

"No," I said, which was a lie. It was early March and getting dark. I'd gone out without a jacket. Of course I was cold. But the relatives hadn't left and I wasn't coming down till they were gone.

"I'm going inside," June said. "Why don't you come

too, Gordy?" Her voice was starting to sound like a mosquito whining in my ear. It made me cross to listen to her.

"Because I don't want to," I said. "Don't tell anybody where I am or I'll bust your butt."

June left. After a while the back door opened. Grandma called into the dark, "Gordon, are you out there?"

I said nothing. Just sat on my branch as if my rear end were frozen to it and waited for her to give up and go inside. Which she soon did.

After that, the relatives' cars began to leave, one by one. I heard Great-aunt Mavis say, "Virginia, you poor thing, promise me you'll take care of yourself. Get some rest or something, cheer up, smile. Nothing's *that* bad, honey."

Little did that skinny witch know about what was bad and what wasn't. She'd never been married to the old man, had she?

I let a few minutes go by, then some more. It was totally dark now, which meant I'd missed "The Shadow," my favorite radio show, and supper, too. The only good thing was, William couldn't see me anymore. Stupid cripple. If he ever got out of that wheelchair and learned to walk, I'd hit him from here to next Sunday.

Finally I climbed down from the tree and went inside. All that was left of supper was the good smell of fried chicken. I helped myself to milk and bread and went up to my room before Grandma saw me. She and the others were too busy laughing at stupid old Jack

Benny to notice me going by the living room door. I guess I could have been lying dead in a ditch somewhere and they wouldn't have cared, as long as they didn't have to turn off the radio and fetch my body.

Before I fell asleep, I heard Grandma coming down the hall to my door. She flipped the light on and took a good look at me. Boy, she just wouldn't leave me alone. I tried rolling over so I couldn't see her but she went right on talking.

"Have you been fighting again, on top of everything else, Gordon?"

I kept my eyes shut, but nothing fooled that old lady. She sat down on the edge of the bed and gave my shoulder a shake. "Playing possum won't help," she said. "Open your eyes and answer me."

"Leave me alone," I said. "I don't want to talk to you or anybody else."

"You certainly were doing some fancy talking to William and Great-aunt Mavis."

"I'm tired now," I said. "I got school tomorrow, I need my rest."

"From what Miss Whipple says about your scholastic achievement, you need more than rest."

The last thing I wanted to do was add Miss Whipple to the things Grandma was mad at me about. "School's harder here," I said. "They're doing decimals already. Mrs. Wagner hadn't started that stuff." Which was a lie. But I figured Grandma wasn't about to make a long-distance call to Mrs. Wagner just to check up on me and my decimals.

Grandma studied my face silently. It made me nervous the way her gray eyes probed mine. So I gave her an ugly look, which she ignored. "Why are you so angry, Gordon?" she asked.

She sounded like she really wanted to know, but I figured it was just an act to soften me up or something. First she'd trick me into a heart-to-heart and then she'd make me apologize to everybody from God on down to William.

When I didn't say anything, she said, "I don't blame you for being mad with Mavis. She had no business talking like that to your mother. But I can't condone rudeness. She's an adult and you're a child. It's not your place to correct her."

If that wasn't the stupidest thing I'd ever heard. A rude adult wasn't any better than a rude child. Worse, actually, because adults, being older, had more practice minding their manners than kids. When I said as much to Grandma, she told me she expected me to write a note to Great-aunt Mavis anyway. "You must tell her you're sorry."

"I'm not sorry and I won't say I am. Lying's worse than being rude."

Grandma pressed her lips together. "How about Mrs. Sullivan's complaint?"

"That crippled kid's mother?"

"Please don't talk about William like that. Don't you have any kindness in your heart?"

"I'm no softy, if that's what you mean. Besides, William's a stuck-up snob. He said I was a moron."

"Tomorrow afternoon you and I will call on the Sullivans," Grandma said. "I'll see to it that you apologize for the language you used."

She got up and walked to the door. Before she left my room, she turned to look at me. "You might want to think about the name William called you. Perhaps he had a reason for using it."

I turned over and punched my pillow. If that didn't beat everything. Moron—William had no call to say I was a moron. I was probably smarter than he was in lots of ways. Book learning's not everything, is it? You have to know how to take care of yourself in this world, and I doubt William knew the first thing about that. Unlike me, he hadn't had the benefit of the old man.

Nine

✧　✧　✧　✧　✧　✧　✧　✧

If there was one thing I learned about Grandma, it was that she kept her word. As soon as I got home from school on Monday, she took me by the arm and hauled me over to the Sullivans' house. I put up a good fight. Made her drag me every step of the way, but she was strong enough to do it.

Grandma must have told Mrs. Sullivan we were coming because the door opened right away. There was snotty William in his wheelchair, trying to look tough but failing miserably. His mother stood beside him in the hall, as fierce as a she-bear with a cub to defend.

"This is my grandson, Gordon Smith," said Grandma. "He's come to tell you he's sorry for his rude behavior."

I didn't look at either one of them. "I'm sorry," I muttered to the floor, wishing I could sink right through the wood, I was so ashamed of myself for giving in to Grandma.

Grandma's grip tightened until her nails bit into my

arm. "Gordon, please look at Mrs. Sullivan and William."

I flashed them the meanest scowl I could muster and returned my gaze to the floor. "I'm sorry."

Those fingernails felt like daggers stabbing me. "This will not do, Gordon. Look Mrs. Sullivan and William in the eye while you apologize. Use their names. Sound as if you mean it."

Lord, Grandma didn't want much, did she? Keeping my eyes as cold and hard as two steel BBs, I stared at William and his mother. Mrs. Sullivan matched me ice for ice but William was smiling, which made me sore as you-know-what. The little cripple was enjoying this. I'd get him later, I thought.

"I'msorryIwasrudeMrsSullivanandWilliam," I said, running the words together so they sounded like the longest vocabulary word any teacher ever invented.

Grandma sighed. "I believe that's the best we can expect, Shirley," she said to Mrs. Sullivan.

I turned to the door, thinking I was free to go, but Grandma didn't loosen her grip on my arm. "Mrs. Sullivan has invited us to sit and visit awhile," she said in that no-nonsense voice of hers. "For some reason, William has expressed an interest in becoming better acquainted with you."

I tried to pull free and run, but Grandma held me all the tighter. I guess she'd expected me to make a break for it.

There was nothing to do but follow Mrs. Sullivan and William into the living room. I sat on the edge of the sofa and looked around. It wasn't the kind of place you could relax in. There were knickknacks everywhere, fancy little china and glass things that would break if you breathed on them. No dust anywhere. No shoes or papers or sweaters scattered around. No toys. The place reminded me of a funeral parlor. The only thing missing was a stiff in a coffin.

A maid brought us a plate decorated with an arrangement of teeny-tiny cookies. She served glasses of milk to William and me. Grandma and Mrs. Sullivan had tea. Everyone but me took tiny bites and little sips. I expected Grandma to say something about my manners, but she was chatting with Mrs. Sullivan about the weather, which was cold for March. William and I just sat there. Even though I wasn't looking at him, I knew he was looking at me. Probably thinking I was a moron who'd been brought up in a barn.

Finally I leaned close to him and whispered, "Quit looking at me."

"I was admiring your black eye," William said. "Who gave it to you?"

"None of your beeswax."

"I bet it was Jerry Langerman."

"Maybe it was Adolph Hitler."

William grinned. "I hope you gave Jerry two black eyes."

I stared at him. "I probably busted his nose."

That actually made William laugh. "Good for you," he said, sounding a lot friendlier. "I hate Jerry. He's the worst kid in Grandville."

Not anymore, I thought, not with Gordy Smith in

town. Compared to me, Jerry Langerman was just some rich doctor's kid cutting up. An amateur juvenile delinquent. I was the real thing.

"I never met anybody with polio before," I said. "Does it hurt?"

William shrugged. "Sometimes."

"Are you going to be crippled all your life?"

"I hope not."

Just then William's mother reached over and patted his head like he was a little pet or something. "William tires easily," she said softly. "Maybe you should say good-bye to Gordon and go lie down, dear."

William frowned. It seemed to me he pulled away just a little bit from his mother's hand. "I'm not tired," he said.

"Yes, you are." His mother went on talking in that soft voice as if she knew more about how William felt than he did. I'd have told her to leave me be if I'd been William, but he just sat there like a prisoner. What he needed was some backbone.

"Can Gordon come back tomorrow?" he asked, not looking at me but at his mother. "We could go up to my room and play with my toys."

"Well," Mrs. Sullivan said slowly, "Gordon might have other things to do, William."

Mrs. Sullivan was giving me an excuse, probably because she was hoping she'd seen the first and last of me. It was real plain she didn't like me. Didn't want me in her house, didn't want me playing with her precious William.

That's all it took to make me say, "I don't mind coming over."

Mrs. Sullivan turned to me. No smile, just as cold-eyed as could be. "You must be careful not to tire William. Excitement's bad for him. He needs rest, peace, quiet."

I figured folks got enough of that when they died, but I just nodded my head like I understood.

Grandma stood up. "Thank you for a lovely treat, Shirley," she said. "I hate to leave, but I have to go home and start dinner." Turning to me, she added, "Tell William good-bye, Gordon. You can talk more tomorrow."

Once we were outside, Grandma said, "Now that wasn't so bad, was it?"

"William's okay," I admitted. "But I don't think his mother likes me."

Grandma gave me one of her looks, but she didn't say anything. Instead she marched me inside, sat me down at the kitchen table, and told me to write that note to Great-aunt Mavis. While she bustled around cooking dinner, I stared at the blank paper. I *was not* going to apologize to that witch. One apology was more than enough for today.

In the living room I heard the gong that meant my second favorite radio show, "Terry and the Pirates," was starting. Next would be "Dick Tracy," then "Jack Armstrong," and "Captain Midnight" after that. I never missed those four shows.

"Can I listen to the radio and then do this?" I asked Grandma. "I got to know what's going to happen to

Terry. Friday he was tied up in this boat that was sinking and—"

Grandma leaned over me. "Write the note first. The faster you do it, the faster you can join the others in the living room."

I scowled at her. "It's not fair. You said yourself that old bag had no business talking to Mama like that."

"I don't remember using words to that effect," Grandma said.

"That was the gist of it."

"Write the note, Gordon. Now."

"You're worse than Hitler and Hirohito and Mussolini all rolled into one."

I thought for sure she'd slap me for that but she just said, "I don't care what you think of me. Write the note."

Gunshots and shouts came from the radio. Victor said something and June shushed him. The music got fast and scary. It sounded like Terry was in real trouble, but even though I strained my ears I couldn't quite hear what was going on.

"Write," Grandma said.

I picked up the pencil. "Deer Grate Ant Maviz," I scrawled. "Im sory I was rood. Yor nefue Gordy." I pressed so hard the pencil point broke on the *y* in my name.

Grandma took the note and read it. "Well," she said, looking at me sharp as a hawk, "at least you know how to spell your own name."

I started to leave but she grabbed my arm. "Is this the best you can do, Gordon?"

"I'm a moron, remember?"

"I didn't call you a moron."

"Maybe not, but you did say William might have had a reason for calling me a moron. Which, if you ask me, is the same as saying it yourself."

On the stove, a pot lid began bouncing up and down like the potatoes inside were making one last try to escape. Grandma laid the note down. "Run along, Gordon. We'll write this over again after we eat."

Like heck we would. She said to write an apology and I had. She didn't say anything about spelling and punctuation and all that dumb stuff. But I kept my thoughts to myself. No sense starting an argument. "Terry and the Pirates" was almost over. I'd worry about the stupid note later.

After dinner, Grandma and I spent two hours at the kitchen table, which meant I missed "The Lone Ranger." Not only did she make sure I spelled everything right in Great-aunt Mavis's note, she went over all my schoolwork. Nobody had ever done that before. I swear Mama hadn't cared what I did so long as nobody came to the house to complain. She was too tired out from the little kids and the old man to pay attention to what I did or didn't do in school.

It seemed to me Mama hadn't gotten over those days yet. Since we'd come to Grandville, all she'd done was sit in the living room and listen to the radio. One soap opera after another, starting with "The Romance of Helen Trent" at twelve thirty and going right on till "Young Widder Brown" ended at five and we switched stations for "Terry and the Pirates." That was a total of eighteen shows, each one dumber than the one before.

At first, Grandma did her best to make Mama take what she called "some responsibility." She tried everything from sympathy to yelling, but nothing worked. Mama just said, "Leave me alone, Mother," and went on listening to the radio, her face as blank as a gray sky in winter. She reminded me of pictures I'd seen of soldiers with battle fatigue.

After a couple of weeks, Grandma gave up. She took care of the little kids. Even persuaded Bobby to start using the toilet, which improved the atmosphere considerably.

Grandma also made sure June's dresses were ironed and her hair was braided nice and neat. She kept her shoes polished, too. Never had to nag her about school. June loved her teacher and she was soon reading better than I was. She could do some arithmetic, too. Right from the start, she'd smiled and wagged her tail, and now Grandma was smiling back. And so was everybody else. June even started bringing friends home with her, something she'd never done in College Hill, mainly because nobody's mother allowed their kids near our place. Here in Grandville, it seemed June could do no wrong.

As for me, I got more frowns than smiles both at home and at school. I didn't make any friends, either. Just enemies. But that's what I was used to, so it didn't matter.

One night we were sitting at the kitchen table, just Grandma and me. I was slaving over my arithmetic problems and she was checking my spelling words. Out of the blue, she said, "Did you know your father's on his way to California?"

I stared at her in disbelief. "I thought he was still in jail."

Grandma shook her head. "Your mother got a letter from him yesterday. Didn't she tell you?"

"Mama never tells me anything." I kicked the table leg, sorely vexed to know the old man was free as a bird. "How come they let him out of jail?"

Grandma sighed and took a sip of tea. "Your mother didn't stick around to press charges, Gordon."

Keeping my voice real low, I muttered a string of cuss words. If Grandma heard, she didn't let on.

"He's hoping to find a job in an aircraft plant in Bakersfield," she said, taking as much care as I did to avoid mentioning the old man's name. Not that she had to. We both knew who we were talking about.

"Good for him," I said, kicking the table leg harder.

"Your mother seemed happy to hear from him."

"She's nuts." With that, I slammed my arithmetic book shut and went up to my room. I expected Grandma to call me back. After all, I hadn't finished my homework. But she let me go without a word.

Not bothering to turn on the light, I flung myself on my bed and stared at the ceiling. At least the old man was heading west, not south. Maybe he'd stay in California and forget about us. I sure hoped so.

Ten

About a week after my big apology, I decided to visit William. Mrs. Sullivan opened the door. From the look on her face, you could tell I was the last person she wanted to see, but she invited me in anyway.

"William," she called. "Gordon Smith has come to see you."

"Great," William cried from upstairs. "Bring him to my room."

Mrs. Sullivan led the way toward the stairs. The first thing I noticed was this strange little seat on a track beside the banister.

"What's that thing for?" I asked.

"It's William's way of managing stairs," Mrs. Sullivan said. "He can ride it up or down."

"Can I try it?"

"Absolutely not." Mrs. Sullivan gave me a look that said I'd better keep my hands off William's contraption. "It's not a toy, Gordon."

Too bad it was in plain sight of the living room, I thought. Otherwise I'd have snuck a ride on it anyway.

"You can stay half an hour," Mrs. Sullivan said. "Don't play rough, don't make a lot of noise, and don't excite him. Remember, William's an invalid."

From what Mrs. Sullivan said, it seemed I would have had just as much fun visiting the old folks at the county home. The only difference was, William had toys and the old folks didn't. So I kept my thoughts to myself and followed Mrs. Sullivan to William's room.

William was waiting for me in his wheelchair. He seemed real pleased to see me.

"Here's Gordon," Mrs. Sullivan said as if William was blind as well as crippled. "Remember what I told you, dear."

William frowned. Whatever his mother had said to him was top secret. I guessed it probably had something to do with keeping an eye on me to make sure I didn't steal anything.

Mrs. Sullivan hung around for a few moments, adjusting the window shades and flicking dust off the furniture with a little flowered handkerchief. "Well," she said, trying to sound cheerful, "I guess I'll go down and listen to one of my shows. If you need me, William, just call. I'll keep the radio turned down so I'll be sure to hear you."

"I'll be all right, Mother," William said, watching her go as if he was afraid she might find something else to tidy before she left the room.

After Mrs. Sullivan had gone, I could hardly decide

what to play with first. William had more toys than Sears and Roebuck. Good stuff from before the war like metal cars and trucks. His own radio. Tons of books and comics and games. Collections of stamps and coins.

But best of all was William's Lionel electric train. It had a whistle that sounded like the real thing, and the locomotive puffed smoke from little capsules you dropped in the stack. Its wheels went *clickety-clack,* and the freight cars had the right names on the sides— Lackawanna, Great Northern, Union Pacific. The track was a big loop that ran over bridges and through tunnels. There were woods and fields and streams, farm buildings and a town. Crossing signals blinked red and green and little bells rang to warn you the train was coming. It was the best layout I'd ever seen outside of a toy store.

"Let's make it go faster," I said, turning the lever on the control box. Soon the engine was flying around the track, shooting in and out of tunnels and crossing bridges, blowing its whistle like mad.

"Be careful," William said nervously, "you'll wreck it."

Just as he warned me, the train jumped the tracks. Cars shot off in all directions, tumbling end over end. It reminded me of the time a freight train derailed a mile or so from our house in College Hill and the old man went up there and stole a couple of cases of whiskey from a split-open boxcar. He said he'd have taken more if he could have carried it.

"Now look what you did." William sounded as upset as a girl.

I picked up the cars and set them carefully on the tracks. "Nothing broke," I said, almost as relieved as he was. If I'd broken anything, I bet Mrs. Sullivan would have made me pay for it.

"My father bought this train set for me when I was born," William said. "He built the whole layout."

I whistled. "It must've cost a fortune."

William shrugged. Somehow I knew money didn't have anything to do with how he felt about the train.

"Dad died in the war," he told me. "His plane was shot down over Holland way back before I got polio. Sometimes I wonder what he'd think if he came home and saw me in this stupid wheelchair. . . ."

William's voice trailed off. Scared he was going to start crying, I began talking about Donny. "My brother's in the infantry somewhere in Germany, but he's not supposed to say exactly where. He was in the Battle of the Bulge and a bunch of other stuff."

William drew in his breath. "You must be worried about him."

I shook my head. "Donny says no stinking German is going to kill him. He's too mean to die. Too tough. Kraut bullets bounce right off him." I puffed out my own chest to show him. "Like Superman."

William didn't say anything. He just sat there looking at me as if I was a little kid who believed in Santa Claus or something equally moronic.

"Donny jokes a lot," I muttered. "But he's brave.

Nothing scares him. We're just alike, Donny and me."

William nodded. "He's Batman and you're Robin."

I looked at William, trying to decide how to take that remark. Was he being sarcastic? Or did he mean it? Since I couldn't tell, I picked up the locomotive and spun the wheels, admiring how nice and smooth they worked.

"Mother told me you have another brother," William went on. "She says he's a deserter."

I stared at William, shocked to hear he knew about Stu. "I guess your nosy mother told you about my old man, too," I said, feeling my face burn.

William looked embarrassed. "She didn't say much."

"How much is much?"

He shrugged and fidgeted with the fringe on his blanket. "I guess he's not very nice."

"No kidding." I set the locomotive on the track. "Tell your mother to mind her own beeswax," I added.

Getting to my feet, I went to the window and looked out into the branches of Grandma's tree. "How come you were spying on me those times?"

William rolled his chair to the window. "I wanted to see what you looked like. Mother told me you were coming to stay with Mrs. Aitcheson, so I—" He broke off with a shrug. "Maybe I'm just plain nosy."

"Maybe you are." I grinned when I said it. At least William was honest about things.

"I used to climb that tree myself before I got polio," he said. "The branch you always sit on was my favorite thinking place."

I didn't know what to say to that, so I stared down at Grandma's yard. June and Victor were running around, playing some dumb kid game. Ernie was chasing them, crying, "Me, too! Me, too!" Bobby was sitting on the porch steps, sucking his thumb and watching. Grandma hung one pair of overalls after another on the clothesline, telling June to stop shrieking, warning Ernie not to throw the stone he'd picked up, reminding Bobby to go to the toilet.

Only Mama was missing. She was probably sitting inside, listening to one of her soap operas. Sometimes I wondered what she got out of them. Why should she care what happened to Stella Dallas or Ma Perkins or Lorenzo Jones? They weren't real people, they didn't need her, so why was she so interested in them when she didn't give a hang about us? It didn't make sense.

William poked my side to get my attention. "You're lucky to have such a big family," he said. "I wish I had a brother or a sister."

"Which one do you want?" I asked, amazed anyone would be envious of my family. "You can have them cheap. A couple of dollars apiece. All except June— she's not for sale."

William laughed, but I swear if he'd handed me a dollar bill I'd have sold him Bobby on the spot.

"That's your window right there, isn't it?" William pointed at the one facing us. I studied it for a minute. He was right, it was mine. I hadn't even noticed.

"Our houses are so close we could talk to each other

at night," William said. "When we're supposed to be asleep."

"I guess so," I said, though I wasn't sure what we'd say to each other.

Before Mrs. Sullivan came up to tell me it was time to leave, William let me run the train again. This time I kept the speed down. No wrecks.

Eleven

❖ ❖ ❖ ❖ ❖ ❖ ❖ ❖

As the weeks passed, Mrs. Sullivan grew used to seeing my ugly face at the door. But she didn't seem to like me any better. Or trust me. I swear to God I half-expected her to check my pockets every time I left her house.

Strange as it sounds, no matter how his mother felt or what she said about me, William seemed to like me. Even more strange, considering how different he was from my old buddies Toad and Doug, I liked William. In fact, he was the only friend I had in Grandville. No matter how much I tried to horn in on Langerman's gang, none of them warmed up to me. They made it pretty clear I was a no-good Northerner, a damn Yankee. The only good thing was, they got tired of fighting me. Instead they just ignored me. Which in some ways was just as bad. Maybe even worse.

One Thursday in April, William and I were in his

room, making model airplanes. He was much better at it than I was. The tissue paper stuck to my fingers, the balsa wood struts broke, the fuselage I built was lop-sided, and the wings kept falling off. My P-47 wouldn't have been any threat to the Luftwaffe, that's for sure. But William's looked ready to shoot the Krauts out of the sky.

While we worked, we listened to the radio. Suddenly "The Green Hornet" was interrupted by a news flash so terrible neither William nor I could believe it. President Roosevelt was dead. A cerebral hemorrhage. At Warm Springs, Georgia. 4:35 in the afternoon.

We stared at each other, speechless. FDR had been president our whole entire lives. He couldn't be dead, he just couldn't.

"Maybe it's a hoax," I said, "like that radio show about the Martians invading earth. 'The War of the Worlds'—remember that?"

"Nobody'd joke about FDR dying," William said, but he let me change the radio station just in case I was right.

I turned the knob from one end of the dial to the other, but the same news was on every station. It was no joke. FDR was dead. Our new president was Harry S. Truman. How could that be? Why, the war wasn't even over. How could we beat Hitler and Hirohito without FDR?

William stared at the radio. Tears ran down his face. "I can't believe it," he whispered. "I can't believe it, I just can't believe it." He was clutching his plane so tightly the balsa frame snapped like tiny gunshots.

"Me, either." I jumped to my feet. "I have to go home, have to tell Grandma."

I passed Mrs. Sullivan on the stairs. For a second, I thought she was going to hug me, but she ran past, rushing up to William.

At home, Grandma was sitting alone by the radio, weeping. I lingered in the doorway, hoping she'd notice me, maybe invite me to sit with her and mourn the president, but if she saw me she gave no sign. I went up to my room and lay down on my bed. It was like God had died and there was nobody to protect us from our enemies.

At dinner that night, Mama got into a fight with Grandma. It started when Grandma said, "I haven't felt grief like this since your father died, Virginia. It's as if FDR were a member of the family, someone I knew personally."

Mama shrugged. "If you ask me, we're better off without him. That New Deal of his almost ruined this country."

Too shocked to say a word, I stared at Mama. How could she say such awful things about the best president we'd had since Abraham Lincoln? Especially on the very day he died?

Grandma leaned across the table, her face fiery red with anger. "How can you say something so stupid,

Virginia? The New Deal brought us out of the Depression. If it hadn't been for FDR—"

"Bunk." Mama looked Grandma in the eye. It was the most life she'd shown in a long time, but it was for the wrong cause. "Not everyone shares your liberal ideas. Roger says—"

Grandma's face turned even redder. "I don't give a damn what Roger says. I won't hear his name mentioned in this house!"

Mama glared at Grandma. "I'll say his name as often as I like! Roger's my husband!"

"And a fine one he turned out to be. Just look at you. Seven children and no way to provide for them. You haven't got the sense of an alley cat!"

Bobby started to cry and Ernie joined in, but Victor and June just sat there, staring first at Grandma, then at Mama, and then back again at Grandma. They looked as scared as I felt.

But Mama didn't pay us any mind. She went on hollering in Grandma's face as if somebody had just pulled a gag off her mouth. "You and Daddy always hated Roger. You said he was no-good poor white trash, you said he'd never amount to a hill of beans."

Grandma leaned toward Mama, her eyes gleaming with spite. "I was right, wasn't I?"

Mama fished a letter out of her dress pocket and thrust it at Grandma. "Read this. Roger's got a good job at a defense plant in Bakersfield. He's working overtime so he can bring us out to California this summer. He's quit drinking, Mother."

Stunned speechless, I gaped at Mama. Surely she hadn't forgotten what a liar he was.

Grandma glanced at the creased and re-creased piece of paper lying beside her plate. From the look on her face, you'd think she was contemplating a dead rat. "I don't believe a word of it, Virginia."

Mama threw her napkin on the table and got up so fast her chair turned over. "You'd better believe it. Come July, we'll be on our way to California. All six of us."

Snatching the letter, Mama left the room. Bobby ran after her but the rest of us stayed put, too shocked to move.

"Is Daddy coming here, Grandma?" June whispered.

"That man wouldn't dare cross my threshold," Grandma said. "If he did, I swear I'd shoot him full of buckshot with your grandpa's old hunting rifle."

Grandma began clearing the table. June followed her out to the kitchen. I heard her say, "You wouldn't really shoot Daddy, would you?"

"I doubt he'll give me the chance," Grandma said.

Not long after I went to bed, I saw William's flashlight blinking SOS. Save Our Souls, our special signal to talk. Easing up my window, I pressed my face against the screen so I could hear him.

"Do you think FDR died because he had polio?" William asked.

"Don't you remember what the man on the radio

said? FDR had a cerebral hemorrhage. It didn't have anything to do with polio, William."

"That's what Mother said, but still . . ." William's voice trailed off as if he wasn't convinced. I guess if I'd been in his shoes, I'd have been scared too.

"I bet worrying about the war killed him," I told William. "It wore his brain out. That's why he got the hemorrhage."

William thought about that for a while. "Do you think we can win the war without him?"

"I hope so," I said, "but it's a shame he won't be here to see us do it. It doesn't seem fair. Him missing the parades and the celebrations."

"Maybe he'll see everything from heaven," William said slowly. "FDR and all the men who died in the war. They'll look down at Earth and they'll be happy we won."

I knew William was picturing his father up there with the president and the angels and God, so I nodded as if I agreed. It was nice to think of all the dead soldiers strolling along streets of gold, laughing and telling jokes the way they used to before Hitler and Hirohito came along and ruined the world.

But to tell you the truth I'm not sure I believe in heaven. It's a swell idea but hard to picture. Why would God be so mean to people while they're alive and then give them cities of gold after they die?

Just then Mrs. Sullivan hollered, "William, turn off that flashlight and go to bed. You have all day tomorrow to talk to Gordon."

William shone his flashlight up into the sky like a searchlight and I pretended to machine-gun a couple of Messerschmitts. *Ackety-ackety-ackety*. Die, evil Nazi, die!

After William shut his window, I went back to worrying about the old man. I wished I could have found the words to tell William what he was really like and how much he scared me. But I doubted William could imagine a boy being afraid of his own father.

To keep from thinking about the old man, I tried reading a comic book. When that didn't work, I tried daydreaming about hopping a freight and heading for the Gulf Stream waters and the redwood forest. I even tried counting backward from a hundred, a trick Stu once taught me.

But every time I shut my eyes, I saw the old man behind the wheel of his old black car, driving east, the morning sun in his eyes, a stubble of whiskers on his chin, a whiskey bottle in the glove compartment. Getting closer every day. Bringing misery with him like an extra passenger.

Twelve

❖ ❖ ❖ ❖ ❖ ❖ ❖ ❖

The next day, I found Mama sitting on the porch swing. She had Bobby on her lap. He slumped against her, sucking his thumb, his face as blank as hers. I sat down beside her but she didn't even look at me. Mama and I never had gotten into the habit of talking.

For a while we just rocked back and forth, slow and gentle. Finally I forced myself to say what was on my mind. "Is the old man really coming here this summer?"

Mama frowned. "Don't be so disrespectful, Gordy. He's your father, not your old man."

"Is he coming or isn't he?"

"Yes, he is," she said, giving me the fiercest look I'd ever seen. Hugging Bobby so tight he squirmed, she glanced at the open living room window and whispered, "We should be in our own home where we can do things our way, not Mother's."

"Our way?" I braced my feet against the porch floor and stopped the swing. Jarred out of her thoughts, Mama looked at me.

"Our way?" I repeated. "Do you mean being shoved down the stairs, having your arm busted, making up lies to protect him? That might be your way, Mama, but it sure isn't my way!"

Mama's face hardened. "You heard what I told Mother. Your father's changed, he's quit drinking, things won't be like before."

I grabbed her arm and made her look at me. "Don't believe him, don't let him come here," I begged. "He's lying, Mama—"

Mama interrupted me. "Gordy, you don't know your father. Not how he was when I first met him. If you could have seen him then . . ." Her voice trailed off as if she was fading away into a dream.

I touched her arm to bring her back. "What was he like, Mama?" I asked, wishing she'd tell me something that would change my mind about the old man. Something that would allow me to believe he might be okay after all.

"Oh, he was just the handsomest man I ever saw," Mama said. "All the girls were mad about him. Even though he was a little wild."

I stared at her, waiting for her to go on. So far, she hadn't said a thing that made sense. "Was he nice to you?" I asked finally.

She smiled. "Of course he was."

"What made him change?"

Mama sighed. "Things went wrong for him after we got married, Gordy. He had bad luck getting jobs. Never found a fair boss. Other men got raises, but not him. He'd ask why and they'd say he had a bad attitude. Or they'd pick on him for some little thing he did wrong, like coming in late or having a couple of beers at lunch."

Mama paused to shift Bobby to her other knee. "The men Roger worked for weren't fit to clean his shoes," she went on. "The way they treated him was just disgraceful."

Bobby began squirming. "Want to get down," he whined.

Mama held him tighter. "You sit still and be good," she whispered, "and Mama will take you to the store for a Popsicle."

Bobby leaned back and stuck his thumb in his mouth.

"Every time your daddy lost a job, he got more unhappy," Mama said. "That's why he started drinking, Gordy. He needed something to cheer him up, make him forget. I can't blame him for it. Life's been hard on him."

"I guess you can't blame him for hitting us," I said, "not with a sad life like that." I was being sarcastic, but Mama didn't notice.

"You know how sorry he was afterward," she said. "He'd give me flowers and perfume just like he did when he first came courting."

"He never gave *me* anything," I said. "Never gave

Stu or Donny anything either. Unless you count black eyes and broken arms and cuts and bruises."

Mama glared at me. "I told you he's changed, Gordy. He won't lay a hand on any of us again. He swore he wouldn't."

That did it. I went hot all over. "Mama, he says the same thing every time he hits you. How can you keep on believing him? Are you crazy or just plain stupid?"

Bobby's thumb fell out of his mouth and he started crying. At the same moment, Mama slapped me hard enough to make my eyes sting. Maybe she had a right to, maybe I had it coming for calling her stupid and crazy, but I was too mad to apologize. She hadn't said one word that convinced me the old man had changed.

Without looking at her, I jumped out of the swing and ran. Out the gate and down the sidewalk, past William's house, past the park, past the corner grocery, past the school and the post office with the flag flying at half-mast for President Roosevelt.

I wanted to run right out of Grandville, but by the time I crossed the train tracks, I was out of breath, stumbling and tripping over my own feet. I kept going, though, till the paved road turned to dirt. Finally I came to a stop under a big tree and flung myself down in the grass.

For a while I just lay there listening to my heart pound. My conversation with Mama played in my head like a scratched record. If she went to California with the old man, she'd go without me. I'd keep my sister and brothers here, too. Maybe Mama and the old man deserved each other, but we kids sure didn't deserve them.

I don't know how long I lay in the grass. The air was warm but the ground still held some of winter's cold and damp. After a while I started feeling stiff. It occurred to me I might be getting polio. That's how it started. Stiffness in the neck and back, weakness in the legs and arms. I sat up real cautiously and tested my arms and legs and neck, turning them this way and that. They seemed to be working okay.

I walked slowly back to Grandma's, hoping to run into Langerman. I pounded my right fist into my left palm—*pow!* That's what I'd do to his ugly kisser if I got the chance.

Which I didn't. Instead of fighting Langerman, I had to content myself with kicking a stone all the way home. Maybe it was just as well. The mood I was in, I'd probably have broken every bone in his body.

Thirteen

✧ ✧ ✧ ✧ ✧ ✧ ✧

For several days, Mama didn't speak to Grandma or me. In fact she didn't have much to say to anybody except Bobby. Once I heard her tell him he was her baby. "She's taken the others away from me, but not you, Bobby. You're still mine."

It made me cold all up and down my backbone to hear Mama talk like that. Grandma hadn't taken us away from her. She'd just treated us nice, that's all. Paid us some attention. Fed us. Talked to us. Wiped Victor's nose, washed Ernie's face, braided June's hair and ironed her dresses.

When Mama finally started speaking to me again, it was mainly to ask for the butter or the bread. She never apologized for slapping my face. Didn't mention the old man to me either, though I heard her speak of him to the others.

It riled me the way Mama talked; she made the old man sound like a cross between Santa Claus and Uncle

Sam, with a little bit of Jesus thrown in for good measure. Right before my eyes I saw Victor, Ernie, and June slowly drift toward believing in this Daddy Mama had made up. The real old man, the one they'd been so scared of, was fading from their memories. If I tried to make them remember, they said he'd changed, he was nice now, Mama said so.

"Ha" was what I said to their pitiful beliefs. Not that that changed anything. After a while I gave up trying and kept my thoughts to myself.

One night I happened to be in the living room when Grandma was reading *Heidi* to June. Although I pretended not to listen, I got sort of interested in the story. It had a lot of dumb, preachy parts, but I liked hearing about Peter and the goats and the old grandfather toasting cheese on the fire and stuff like that.

This particular evening, Grandma was reading about a crippled girl named Clara who'd come to stay with Heidi. Peter was jealous of Clara, so he pushed her empty wheelchair down the mountain where it smashed to pieces. Good-o for Peter, I thought.

He did it to make Clara go back to the city, but busybody Heidi talked the grandfather into carrying Clara up the mountain so she could see the pretty flowers. While they were in the meadow, Heidi got this bright idea to teach Clara to walk again. She bossed poor old Peter (who was scared he was going to jail because of breaking the wheelchair) into helping.

While Grandma read, I kept my head bent over the planes and tanks I was drawing, but I paid close attention. Clara reminded me of William, scared of trying things. His mother hung all over him just like Clara's grandmother hung all over her.

Grandma got to the part where Clara's grandmother comes to visit. She sees Heidi help Clara to her feet, and she almost dies of fright. But then she realizes Heidi has taught Clara to walk and she runs to them, laughing and crying, and hugs them and kisses them and makes a big fuss over everybody, even the goats.

When Grandma came to the end of the chapter, June asked if Clara had polio. "Is that why she couldn't walk?"

"Maybe," Grandma said, closing the book.

"But Clara got well," June said, sighing happily. "She drank fresh milk and she slept in the hay like Heidi and she saw the stars. Heidi and Peter and the grandfather taught her to walk again. She didn't need the wheelchair anymore. Isn't that nice, Grandma?"

Grandma gave my sister a little hug and got to her feet. "Time for bed, June. You too, Gordon."

"Where's Mama?" June asked.

"On the porch, I guess."

Grandma and June went on upstairs, but I rolled over on my back and stared at the ceiling. The story had given me an idea. Suppose I taught William to walk again? We'd do it like Heidi did—keep it a secret and surprise his mother.

I pictured Mrs. Sullivan running to hug and kiss

William and me, laughing and crying like Clara's grandmother. She'd say, "Why, Gordy Smith, all this time I thought you were heading for reform school, but I was wrong about you, so wrong. I can never thank you enough!"

Just then, Grandma walked into the living room and saw me sprawled on the carpet where she'd left me. "I thought I told you to go to bed, Gordon."

"Yes ma'am." I got to my feet, shoved *Heidi* under my shirt, and left the room before she noticed I had the book.

As I passed the front door, I glanced outside. Sure enough, Mama was sitting in the porch swing, rocking slowly back and forth. I could see the red tip of her cigarette glowing in the dark. Its smoke mixed with the smell of honeysuckle and fresh-cut grass. If she saw me standing there, my face pressed against the screen, she didn't say anything.

I went on upstairs, one step at a time, dragging myself along by the railing as if I was learning to walk all over again.

The next afternoon I went over to William's. I'd stayed up half the night skimming through Heidi, finding all the parts about Clara. It seemed walking hurt her feet at first, but I figured William was tough enough to stand a little pain if it meant saying good-bye to his wheelchair.

Mrs. Sullivan actually said we could play in the yard. Poor William was so excited you'd have thought we were going on a safari. First his mother bundled him up in a thick sweater and made him promise to keep his cap on. Then she eased his wheelchair down the steps and pushed him to a tree where she could watch us from the kitchen window.

After Mrs. Sullivan left, William and I played war for a while. At first we were pilots. I'd taught William how to make airplane and bomb sounds and he'd gotten almost as good at it as I was. Then we were soldiers like Donny, machine-gunning Nazis and throwing hand grenades. I was badly wounded but I managed to drag myself out of range and fire some mortar rounds from behind William's wheelchair, which was the tank. He was the gunner. He blew up three Panzers and a half track and shot down six Nazi planes. There were dead Krauts everywhere. General Patton gave us both the Congressional Medal of Honor. He said we were the finest and bravest soldiers he'd ever had the pleasure of meeting.

"Maybe your brother Donny will really get a medal," William said when we'd gotten tired of playing war.

I was making a whistle out of a blade of grass, something Stu had taught me. "Oh, he'll win a dozen medals, maybe more," I said. "He's so brave he'll probably win a whole chest full. In fact, he'll have to hire somebody to wear the ones that won't fit on his uniform."

I grinned at the idea of Donny swaggering through the front door, weighed down with medals. A hero, that's what he'd be. Just the kind of soldier I'd be if I ever went to war.

I blew a loud blast on my whistle and rolled over on my back to see William. "Don't you get sick of being in that wheelchair?"

William gave me a startled look, kind of like a rabbit who hadn't noticed a cat sneaking up on him till it was almost too late. "What do you think?" he asked, sounding hurt I'd ask such a dumb question.

"I bet you could walk if you really wanted to."

William shook his head sadly. "No, I can't. Mother says—"

I hushed him. "Your mother watches over you too close, William. She's holding you back. You've got to stand up to her."

"That's easy for you to say," William muttered, turning his face away as though he wanted me to stop talking.

But I didn't intend to stop. No, sir. Not till I convinced him. "All you need is a little gumption and you'll be on your feet again."

He stared at me. "Do you really think so?" His voice had a little quaver of hope in it.

"Remember what FDR said? 'All we have to fear is fear itself.'" Leaning closer to William, I added, "*He* didn't just sit around in a wheelchair feeling sorry for himself, you know."

To keep from looking at me, William fidgeted with the fringe on his blanket and shook his head. "My mother says—"

With my face an inch from his, I forced him to meet my eyes. "I don't care what your mother says. Just try.

[86]

You can do it, I know you can. In fact—" I shoved my face even closer. "I'll help you, William."

"Mother won't let you help me," he said uneasily. "She won't even let you take me around the block in the wheelchair."

I kicked at the pile of acorn bombs we'd made. "Your mother hates me."

William's face got red and he went back to fidgeting. "Of course she doesn't hate you," he mumbled.

"You're a lousy liar, William, but it doesn't matter, I don't care. I'm used to people hating me. They always do. Grown-ups, I mean. Teachers, other kids' parents." I spit in the grass to show him what I thought of adults in general.

I looked up just in time to see Mrs. Sullivan walking toward us. The look on her face told me she'd seen me spit and hadn't much liked it. How I wished I could pry William away from that woman. Heidi was lucky to live high in the mountains far from Clara's fussy grandmother.

"Promise you'll think about it," I whispered in William's ear.

He nodded, but his mother was beside him now, making it impossible for him to say anything. "It's time to go inside, William," she said. "You look pale and tired. I think you've had enough excitement for one day."

Turning to me, she added, "Run along home, Gordon. We'll see you tomorrow."

I left the Sullivans' yard but instead of going inside,

I scrambled up into the tree and perched on my favorite branch. It was strange to think William had sat here once. He'd been strong like me. He could do everything a regular kid did—climb trees, play in the creek, ride a bike, go to school. Then all of a sudden he got polio and couldn't do anything.

Actually it was more than strange—it was down-right scary to think how fast William's life had changed.

I swung out of the tree, promising myself to get William back on his feet even if I had to break his wheelchair to do it. A little encouragement from me, a little effort on his part. That's all it would take.

Fourteen

❖ ❖ ❖ ❖ ❖ ❖ ❖

Every time I went over to William's, I brought up the walking idea, but, no matter how hard I tried, I couldn't sell him on it. He'd just sit in that stupid old wheelchair of his and say, "I can't, I can't, I can't." Sometimes I'd get so mad I'd go home in a huff and not come back for two or three days.

One afternoon I brought *Heidi* with me and asked him if he'd ever read it. Of course he had. William has read just about every book written, including *Moby-Dick*. I'm not talking about the Classic Comic either. He read the real thing, all five or six hundred pages. Didn't skip a single word. Not even the long boring chapter about whales. That's how smart he was.

I opened *Heidi* to the part about Clara and handed it to him. "Look at this."

William glanced at the picture of Clara walking into her grandmother's arms while Heidi watched, grinning like crazy.

"If Clara could learn to walk again, you can, too," I said. "All you have to do is try. T-R-Y."

Miss Whipple had just said the same thing to me that afternoon about my multiplication tables. I hadn't believed her, so don't ask me why I expected William to believe me. I guess I was desperate.

"Clara's a girl in a book," William said, sounding scornful. "She's not real, Gordy. The writer made her up."

"I know that." I scowled at him. "I might not be as smart as you, but I'm not stupid either."

I felt like adding, "Besides, I can walk," but I kept my mouth shut. It was time to go home for dinner anyway.

The next day the news we'd all been waiting for finally came. The principal himself ran into our classroom and shouted, "Boys and girls, the Germans have surrendered! The war in Europe is over!"

You never heard such a commotion in your life. We jumped to our feet, yelling and hollering and dancing like crazy people. Girls cried, they were so happy. So did teachers. Even Langerman and I forgot we hated each other. It was one of the happiest moments of my whole entire life. And, to top it off, school closed early and we all ran home, screaming and laughing.

We'd been expecting it, of course. For weeks the Allies had been rolling through Germany so fast nothing could stop them. Not Nazi guns, not Nazi tanks, not what was left of the Luftwaffe.

Not even Hitler himself. When he finally realized he

was losing the war, he'd killed himself and so had a bunch of other Nazis, including Goebbels. Some took poison, some shot themselves. Cowards every one of them, scared to face what they'd done to the world and their own country.

Frankly, I'd hoped to see those Nazis shot or hanged. Maybe even tortured the way they tortured other people. Or at least shot and hung upside down in a square like Mussolini.

Neither William nor Grandma agreed with me—they both thought I was bloodthirsty. But so what? The Nazis deserved the worst we could give them for the stuff they did. The pictures in *Life* magazine proved that—all those dead Jews in the concentration camps.

Anyway, that afternoon William was waiting for me on the front porch, grinning and holding up the newspaper to show me a headline a blind man could have read, it was so big and black: NAZIS QUIT.

We read the paper together. It seemed the war in Europe had lasted five years, eight months, and six days. That's a total of 2,076 days, beginning on September 1, 1939, when Hitler invaded Poland and started it all, and ending on May 7, 1945. In that time, *The Grandville Sentinel* said, forty million people had been killed, wounded, or captured. Civilians as well as soldiers. Old people, mothers, kids, babies. Jews who died in concentration camps worse than anything in hell. Towns bombed to rubble, crops destroyed, farm animals slaughtered. Which meant no homes, no food. All because of Hitler.

While I was reading, I glanced at William and caught

him staring at the gold star in his window. It gave me a lump in my throat to imagine what he was thinking. The soldiers would be coming home soon, including Donny, but William's father wouldn't be with them. That had to be tough for him. And his mother, too.

"Daddy was a hero," William said softly. "He died for his country. But I wish he hadn't, I wish he was coming back with the other pilots."

I patted his shoulder, thinking of people I'd known in College Hill who wouldn't be coming back from the war either—Butch, Jimmy, Harold. Others, too: kids' fathers and uncles and brothers. All dead because of Hitler. I cussed that Nazi good, which shocked William, but I didn't care.

"When do you think your brother will come home?" William asked.

"Donny? Soon, I hope. He's been over there since just after D-Day."

"I heard the longer you've been in Europe the sooner you can leave," William said.

"Sounds fair to me," I said.

"Unless they decide to send you to the Pacific," William added.

That got me to cussing Tojo worse than I'd cussed Hitler.

The next day was a holiday. V-E Day—Victory in Europe. School was closed but a lot of people were too worried to celebrate. After all, the war was only half over. Soldiers and sailors and marines were still dying in the Pacific. It seemed Tojo wasn't ready to give up yet.

After lunch, I went next door to ask Mrs. Sullivan if William could come outside. The grass was growing tall and green and birds were singing and hopping around, building nests and finding food. Blue sky, flowers, sunshine. She couldn't say no.

Mrs. Sullivan pushed William's chair to the tree and gave him the usual warning about getting chilled. Then, looking back once or twice, she went inside.

William and I played war for a while; then we read a couple of new comics he'd bought with his allowance. A breeze stirred the leaves above our heads. The sound made me restless. Tired of sitting still, I climbed the tree and hung upside down from a branch. I crossed my eyes and stuck out my tongue to make William laugh. Then I skinned the cat and dropped down in the dirt beside the wheelchair.

"I wish your mother would let me take you somewhere to celebrate V-E Day," I said.

"Me, too."

We both looked at the house. Faintly, we heard the theme music swell up for "The Right to Happiness," a sappy show about this divorced lady and her dumb little kid, Skippy. It seemed to be coming from my house as well as William's. Our mothers didn't have much in common, but they both listened to the same silly soap operas. In fact, women for miles around were probably getting out their hankies, all set to cry for the next fifteen minutes. Suddenly I got an idea.

"Does your mother listen to 'Backstage Wife,' too?"
I asked.

William was smart enough to guess what I was thinking. "She'll be glued to the radio till 'Young Widder Brown' is over. The world could end and she wouldn't notice."

I got to my feet and quietly pushed William around the house, through the front gate, and down the sidewalk. "Where do you want to go?"

"How about Costello's Drug Store?" William reached into his pocket and showed me his money. "Thirty cents. We can get bubble gum. Cherry Cokes. Good and Plenties. Mother never lets me have stuff like that. She says it's bad for my teeth."

Before we'd gone more than a couple of blocks, I found out pushing a wheelchair was hard work. The farther we went, the heavier William got and the hotter the sun beat down on my head. I had to get him over the curb and back up again every time we crossed a street. I discovered hills I'd never noticed when I was just walking along.

By the time we got to Costello's, I was glad to ease the wheelchair through the screen door and maneuver it down the aisle to the soda fountain in the back. Thanks to the big fan hanging from the ceiling, it was a little cooler inside. But not much.

The lady behind the counter leaned over and grinned down at William. "Bless your heart, I haven't seen you in a coon's age," she said. "You look real good, honey."

William thanked her and ordered two cherry Cokes. He wanted me to hoist him up on a stool, but I couldn't do it. He was just too heavy. So he had to drink his Coke sitting in the wheelchair while I twirled round and round at the counter.

"Who's your friend?" the lady asked William, but she was looking at me, all beady-eyed with curiosity.

"Mrs. Maxwell, meet Gordy Smith," said William. "He's living with his grandmother, Mrs. Aitcheson."

"Well, I'll be," Mrs. Maxwell said, giving me all her attention. "You must be one of Virginia's children. I knew your mama. We went to high school together." She paused to give the countertop a swift wipe with a towel and then added, "I remember when your daddy blew into town. He was a handsome rascal, that's for sure."

Leaning a little closer, she dropped her voice so it sounded solemn, but I could hear nosiness buzzing around my head like a mosquito. "How's your mama, honey? I heard she's here in Grandville, but I haven't seen hide nor hair of her."

"Mama's just fine," I said. Looking her in the eye, I sucked up the rest of my Coke, making as loud a noise as possible.

"You favor Roger," Mrs. Maxwell said. Maybe insulting me was her way of getting even for the noise I was making. "You've got his eyes and coloring."

"I've got my own eyes and my own coloring and I don't favor anyone. Not Mama. Not Roger, either." Giving Mrs. Maxwell one last dirty look, I slid off the stool and grabbed the wheelchair. "Come on, William, we have to go. 'Lorenzo Jones' is just starting."

William took the hint. "Young Widder Brown" came on after "Lorenzo Jones," and it would take us nearly fifteen minutes to get home. Maybe longer, as I wasn't feeling as strong as I had when we started out.

"You be careful, Gordy Smith," Mrs. Maxwell called after us. "I'm surprised Shirley let you bring William all this way."

I let the screen door slam behind me. "Nosy old bag," I muttered, adding a few cuss words just to get William's goat.

"You shouldn't have been so rude, Gordy," said William, sounding like the worrywart he was. "What if Mrs. Maxwell calls Mother and tells her you brought me down here?"

Not being as smart as William, I hadn't thought of that, but it was too late to do anything about old busybody Maxwell now. The important thing was to get William home before his mother noticed he was gone.

Somehow we managed it, even after being chased two blocks by Langerman's chow dog, which probably helped since it surely sped us up. Anyway, when Mrs. Sullivan came outside we were sitting under the tree reading comic books as if we'd been there all afternoon.

"You look hot, Gordon," said Mrs. Sullivan. "Maybe you should go home and lie down for a while. Cool off."

"Yes, ma'am," I said.

Mrs. Sullivan stopped at the clothesline to hang up a basket of laundry. I leaned close to William. "Just think what fun it would be to *walk* to Costello's," I whispered. "You could go anywhere you pleased. Climb trees again. Ride that bike rusting away in your garage. Play in the creek."

William frowned and plucked at his blanket. "There's no sense talking about it, Gordy. I can't, and that's that."

Keeping an eye on Mrs. Sullivan, I went on talking. "We could sneak off to the park every day and practice like Heidi and Clara in the meadow. Imagine how happy your mother would be if one day you just walked through the front gate and up the steps and in the door."

As I talked, I imagined William sauntering along beside me. We'd have our hands in our pockets and we'd be singing the Army Air Corps fight song. It would be sunny and warm like today, a nice breeze, birds singing. The picture was so real I knew it would come true. It just had to.

William smiled like he saw the same picture. "Do you really think I could do it, Gordy? Really and truly? Cross your heart and hope to die?"

"Yes, yes, yes!" I zoomed around his wheelchair making airplane noises. "Off we go," I sang, "into the wild blue yonder, flying high into the sun."

Mrs. Sullivan peered out from behind the sheet she'd just hung up. "I thought you'd gone home, Gordon." Coming closer, she gripped the handle of

William's wheelchair and began pushing him toward the house.

"See you tomorrow, Gordy," William called.

I watched Mrs. Sullivan maneuver the chair up the porch steps. Soon she wouldn't have to do that. William would be running ahead of her, taking the steps two at a time, beating her inside.

Grabbing the limb of my tree, I did a dozen chin-ups and then ran home singing the rest of the fight song.

Fifteen

✧ ✧ ✧ ✧ ✧ ✧ ✧ ✧

T he next afternoon, William and I sat under the tree, waiting for "The Right to Happiness" to begin. When the first throb of organ music floated out the kitchen window, I jumped to my feet. "Let's go, William."

I thought he'd be as excited as I was but he gave me one of his worrywart looks. "Are you sure this is a good idea?"

Instead of answering, I started pushing his wheelchair around the house. William didn't say anything, so I kept going. Out the gate, down the sidewalk, around the corner, heading for Meridian Hill as fast as I could go before William decided to tell me to stop, he'd changed his mind, he didn't want to walk after all.

When we got to the park, I was so hot I thought I might have sunstroke like the English soldiers I once saw in a movie about the Sahara Desert. I wanted to get a drink at the public fountain but William said I'd better not. You never knew who'd drunk before you or what germs they might have left behind. He finished by saying, "Do you want to end up with polio, too?"

"Next time I'll bring a thermos or something," I said, remembering those cherry Cokes at Costello's.

I rolled the wheelchair down a little slope, trying not to think about pushing it back up, and stopped in the nice shady place I'd told William about. There wasn't a soul in sight. The park was as deserted as a meadow in the Alps. I wouldn't have been surprised to see a goat or two grazing on the grass.

Too pooped to do anything else, I flopped down to take a breather.

William stared at me. "What now, Gordy?"

"As soon as I get my strength back, I'll help you stand up. Then we'll take a step or two."

He looked around, smiling like he was enjoying a change of scenery. "This is nice, Gordy. Can't I just sit a while?"

"That's not what we came here for, William. You want to walk again, don't you?"

His hands tightened on the wheelchair's arms. "Yes, but I'm scared it'll hurt."

"It probably will at first," I said, remembering how Clara winced and cried in the beginning. "But you'll get used to it."

"What if I fall?" His voice came out sort of high and wobbly.

"I'll pick you up."

"You're sure I can do it?"

"How many times do I have to tell you? If you try hard enough, you'll walk. Remember—T. R. Y. *Try.*"

I took hold of William's hands. I thought I could just pull him to his feet, but even though William was shorter and skinnier than I was, he seemed to weigh two or three times as much. Maybe it was because he couldn't help lift himself. Anyway, we ended up tipping the chair over. The grass was soft, so it didn't hurt William much when he tumbled out onto the ground.

"Now we have to get you up on your feet," I said.

We struggled and tried and grunted and groaned, but William just couldn't stand up. It seemed easy when Heidi and Clara did it. I couldn't figure out why we were having so much trouble.

"William, you're just not trying," I said at last.

"I am so!" It was the first time he'd ever yelled at me.

"No, you aren't!" I hollered back. "You like sitting around having people wait on you and feel sorry for you and let you have your own way because you're crippled!"

That made William cry. He even tried to hit me, which wasn't easy because he was lying on his face in the grass. "It's not true," he cried. "I'd give anything to walk. I hate being crippled!"

"Prove it," I said. "Stand up and walk!"

"Who the hell do you think you are? Jesus?" William was sweating and his face was all streaked with tears, but he'd stopped crying.

Actually what I'd had in mind was this sergeant I'd

seen in a movie once. He'd been tough on his men because he thought that would make them brave and strong.

"No," I shouted. "I'm just trying to help you, that's all!"

I turned around and walked off. I wasn't really going to leave him. I was faking to see if he'd get so worried he'd get up and come after me.

"Gordy," William screamed, "come back! Don't leave me here!"

I stopped but I didn't turn around. I was still hoping he'd take a step or two in my direction.

"I hate you, Gordy, I hate you! You're nothing but a low-down stinking bully!"

William's voice wasn't any closer than it had been before. Finally I turned around and looked at him. He was still on his stomach, propped up on his arms, trying to drag himself toward me. His face was red and he was crying so hard his snot and tears had mixed together. He was cussing me out, too, using words I'm sure he'd never spoken before in his whole entire life.

Suddenly it hit me like a fist in my guts. William couldn't stand up and walk, no matter how much I wanted him to. No matter how much he himself wanted to. He'd been right all along—Clara was just some girl in a book and so was Heidi. This was real life. Trying to make him walk was the dumbest thing I'd done since I jumped off the roof when I was little, thinking I could fly like Superman.

I ran back to William and tried to calm him down,

but he was so mad I couldn't get through to him. He flailed around and tore up grass and carried on like a crazy person. He kept on swearing like he wasn't ever going to stop. I've got to admit he was better at stringing words together than I was.

At last he wore himself out and lay there. He wouldn't look at me, he wouldn't speak to me.

For a few minutes, I stared down at him, trying to decide what to do. The truth is, I felt like crying too. Finally I took a deep breath and said, "I'm sorry, William, I'm sorry."

It was the first time I'd ever apologized of my own free will. First time I'd ever truly been sorry for anything.

"You were right all along," I added. "It was a dumb idea, and I wish you'd quit being mad."

But no matter what I said, William wouldn't speak or look at me. He had those dry shudders people get when they've cried a long time. Though I'd never experienced them myself, I'd seen June act like that after a bad scene with the old man.

"I know you hate me, William, but I have to get you back home." I set the wheelchair up, glad I hadn't broken it like Peter had, but William kept his head turned. He didn't seem to care if he stayed in the park all night.

I squatted down beside him. "Your mother's going to be looking for you soon," I said. Though I didn't have a watch, I swear I could hear the last notes of the "Young Widder Brown" organ music fading away on radios all over Grandville.

"Leave me alone," William whispered. "Just let me stay here, let me die."

"Don't be stupid." I grabbed him under the arms but he fought me with all the strength he had. Puny as he was, I couldn't seem to drag him to the wheelchair, so I dropped him and pulled the wheelchair close to him.

The sun beat down on me hotter and hotter. Sweat ran down my back. A mosquito buzzed around my head. Gnats bit my ears. Suddenly anger began swelling in my skull like a huge red bubble. If it broke, I'd hit William, I knew I would, I wouldn't be able to stop my self from hitting him. I wanted to hit him and hit him again till he did what I told him to.

I backed away, scared of myself. William just lay where he was. He had no idea what I was thinking.

Somehow I managed to swallow my temper. I swear I could almost taste it. Strong and ugly and thick enough to gag me. I forced myself to uncurl my fists, to remember William wasn't Langerman. He couldn't hit me back. He was little and helpless, like Victor or Ernie.

When I was sure it was safe, I got William under the arms again. He was too tired to fight me, but he sure didn't help. I just about busted a gut getting him into that stupid wheelchair. I felt like a soldier rescuing a wounded buddy, but the only thanks I got from William was a string of cuss words that would have gotten his mouth washed out with soap if his mother had heard them.

He didn't say another word. It didn't matter much because I didn't have breath to waste talking. I thought

I'd die pushing the wheelchair back up the slope to the path. All that kept me going was pretending I was Donny. A Kraut platoon was looking for me. I was ducking mortar fire, outrunning the Nazis, sly as a fox and twice as fast, saving my buddy's life.

The trouble was, I ended up caught behind enemy lines. As I pushed the wheelchair around the corner of our street, heading for the final run right down the middle, who did I see blocking the sidewalk but Mrs. Sullivan and Grandma.

At the sight of his mother, William started crying again, but I kept on going. What else could I do? Mrs. Sullivan gave me a look of such pure hatred I almost dropped dead on the spot. Without saying a word to me, she grabbed the wheelchair and pushed it into her yard.

Before Grandma dragged me home, I saw Mrs. Sullivan lift William out of the chair and carry him inside. He looked at me once, his eyes just as full of hate as his mother's.

Though I expected a beating like I'd never had before, Grandma sent me straight upstairs for a bath. She'd talk to me when I was clean, she said.

For once I didn't argue. A tub full of water might be just the thing to drown myself in. I actually tried submerging like a submarine but I ended up blowing bubbles and surfacing. There was no sense dying yet.

When I was presentable, Grandma sat me down at the kitchen table. Mama was on the back steps watching the little kids play under the sprinkler. I could see her profile from my chair. Every now and then she'd say something like, "Don't be so rough with Bobby, Victor." Or, "Careful, June, don't step on that bee." Ordinary mother things.

"I'd like to hear your side of this, Gordon," said Grandma.

I glanced at her, surprised she didn't sound mad. She wasn't screaming or threatening me or anything. But I supposed I'd soon find myself traipsing next door to apologize again to Mrs. Sullivan and William.

"I was just trying to help," I mumbled. "I know it sounds dumb, but I thought I could teach William to walk. Like Heidi helps Clara in that stupid book you read to June."

Grandma sighed. "Shirley says William is very delicate. She doesn't think he'll ever walk again. Lacks the strength. Sometimes I wonder, though. Shirley's so protective, so fearful. Maybe if she . . ." Grandma stopped and shook her head. "Just leave William alone, Gordon."

"But if he really tried—"

"He's doing the best he can," Grandma put in.

I hung my head. "I know he is, but . . ."

"But what?" Grandma asked when I let my sentence trail off unfinished.

I shrugged. The thing was, I couldn't imagine wanting to do something and not being able to. Even math and all that other boring school stuff. If I truly wanted to figure percentages and change decimals into fractions, I probably could. I just didn't want to. So I didn't try. It was as simple as that. Wasn't it?

"William hates me now," I said. "And I don't even know why." To my complete disgust, tears welled up in my eyes. When one splashed on the table, I wiped it away fast with my thumb, hoping Grandma wouldn't see. I'd never cried about anything in my whole life and I didn't want to start now.

Grandma was silent a moment. "Maybe William believed you," she said at last. "Maybe you convinced him he could walk if he tried hard enough. And then he couldn't after all."

I pictured William lying there in the grass, trying to pull himself along by his arms, red-faced, sweating, cussing me. I also remembered how I'd wanted to hit him. I couldn't tell Grandma that. "Do you think he'll ever forgive me?"

This time Grandma was quiet for so long I thought she'd fallen asleep or something. "Forgiving's not easy," she said at last. "I guess that's why so many people leave it up to God."

I looked at her sharply, wondering if she was thinking about the old man. I doubt even God had enough mercy in his heart to forgive *him*.

If she guessed my thoughts, Grandma didn't let on. "Come help me shell peas for dinner," she said, patting my hand. "It'll take your mind off William for a while."

Grandma and I sat at the table side by side. Peas pinged into the bowl. Outside, the little kids shrieked and laughed. Once Mama laughed too.

After a while I asked Grandma if she was going to make me go next door and apologize to Mrs. Sullivan.

She shook her head. "I don't think she wants to see you anytime soon, Gordon. I'll explain what you were trying to do and tell her how sorry you are. Maybe that will help."

When I went to my room that night, I sat on the edge of my bed for a long time staring at William's house. I hadn't smoked once since I'd come to Grandma's, but I'd have given anything for a cigarette now. If Mama wasn't so careful of her Luckies, I'd have stolen one, but she carried them in her pocket. Never left them lying around. I guess that's what shortages do to people. Make them into misers. Well, maybe when the war was over I'd have all the cigarettes I wanted.

I tried shining my flashlight at William's window to see if he'd come and talk but he didn't. Not even when I clicked the light off and on in our special code—SOS, SOS.

Finally I gave up and used my flashlight to read the Hardy Boys book William had loaned me back in the good old days when we were friends. He owned the whole set and he'd been letting me borrow them one by one. This was the best yet, and I was sorry I couldn't talk to him about it. We could have acted it out in his backyard if I hadn't made him hate me forever.

Sixteen

❖ ❖ ❖ ❖ ❖ ❖ ❖ ❖

For a couple of days, I kept an eye on William's house—even sat in the tree for hours to get a good view of his yard—but he didn't come outside. He didn't spy on me from behind his window curtain, either. Finally Grandma told me he and his mother had gone to visit relatives in the country. Mrs. Sullivan had said they needed a change of scene—which probably meant they needed to get away from me.

I told myself William was just a dumb old cripple and I was tired of sitting around his house. But it wasn't true. He was my best and only friend and I really missed him. Without William, there was absolutely nothing to do and nobody to talk to except June. And I couldn't count on her because she was almost always playing with a silly, giggly girl named Nancy who lived down the street.

Not long after school let out for the summer, something happened that cheered me up, at least for a while.

Donny came home. He just showed up at the front door one hot afternoon in July. Hadn't told anyone he was coming. Wanted to surprise us, he said.

I swear I hardly knew him. Maybe it was his uniform, but he seemed different. Taller, skinnier—older. Not just three years older, but some other kind of older I didn't understand.

Mama seemed happy to see him. She hugged him and kissed him and told him he looked "just like your daddy when he was your age."

That wiped the smile off Donny's face fast enough, but Mama didn't notice. She was calling the little kids inside, telling them their big brother was home. "Donny," she said. "It's Donny. Don't you remember?"

The boys hung back like a litter of puppies huddling together for safety, but June flung her arms around Donny and carried on as if he was her hero.

All the while everybody, including Grandma, was making a fuss over Donny, I was stealing looks at his duffel bag, wondering if he'd brought home souvenirs. I was hoping for a Nazi helmet. Or an Iron Cross. I'd seen Langerman wearing both last week. He said his cousin had given them to him. Bragging as usual, making me so sore I wanted to punch him. Would have if his mother hadn't come along in her car and picked him up.

"Did you kill lots of Krauts?" I asked when I had a chance. "Was the Battle of the Bulge as bad as they say? What was Berlin like? Did you see the bunker where Hitler killed himself? Do you think he's really dead?"

I was leading Donny upstairs, carrying the duffel bag fosr him, wanting to know everything he'd seen and done over there.

"Did you get any medals?" I went on, lugging that bag up a step at a time, feeling the weight of it pulling my arms out of their sockets. "Where are they? Can I see them?"

At the door of the bedroom Grandma said he could have, Donny took the duffel bag. "Thanks, Gordy," he said, and shut the door in my face.

"Hey," I shouted. "Tell me what you did, Donny. What was it like? Did you bring home some Nazi helmets?"

There was no answer. I banged on the door. "Let me in, Donny, I want to talk to you, I want—"

"Leave your brother alone." Grandma grabbed my arm. I hadn't even heard her coming. "He's tired—he's been on a train for hours, all the way from New York. And a ship before that. He'll talk to you when he feels like it."

"But—"

"No buts." Grandma led me away.

Donny came downstairs at dinnertime. He'd changed his clothes. In a sport shirt and khaki pants, he looked ordinary. Not like a vet or anything special. Just some guy who might have spent the whole war in Grandville.

I tried asking more questions but Donny didn't answer a single one of them. You'd think he'd gone deaf.

"You wouldn't understand, Gordy," he said at last.

"You weren't there. Now shut up and let me eat my dinner."

That was the whole point. I wasn't there, I didn't understand, but how would I ever know if he didn't tell me? I opened my mouth to argue, but Grandma gave me a warning look. Then Mama started telling Donny about the old man's job in Bakersfield.

"They plan to convert the plant after Japan surrenders," she said. "They'll manufacture other things for peacetime. Radios and electrical stuff. So Roger will keep his job."

Donny raised one eyebrow, but all he said was, "That's good, Ma, that's real good. But what's it got to do with us?"

"He's your father, Donny," said Mama, as if there was some chance the war had made my brother forget.

Donny sipped his iced tea. "So?"

Mama's face flushed. "He's getting a house for us. He'll be coming here in August. We'll go back to California with him then. All of us."

I noticed Mama emphasized the part about all of us going, even though I'd already told her to count me out.

Grandma sighed but she didn't say anything. Like me, she'd given up trying to argue Mama out of her foolishness.

Donny set his glass down and stared at Mama. His face was as hard as mine felt. "You must be nuts."

Without waiting for her to answer, he got up and left the room. A few seconds later, the front door slammed. Then the front gate. I watched Donny walk past the house and disappear into the summer evening.

We all looked at his plate. He'd eaten just about half his dinner.

"I thought he'd be pleased," Mama said.

"Apparently you thought wrong," said Grandma. Turning to June, she said, "Eat your chicken. You need some meat on your bones."

June made a face at the chicken, but she ate it. She knew better than to say no to Grandma.

I don't know when Donny came home that night. I fell asleep waiting for him. But the next morning I found him on the back steps, drinking a bottle of beer and smoking a cigarette. I sat down beside him and asked if I could have a drag.

"Hell, no," he said.

"I smoke," I said. "I even know how to inhale."

"Get your own cigarettes then. I'm not giving you any."

"Will you tell me about the war, then?"

"Can't you get it through your thick skull? There's nothing to tell you."

I didn't like his tone of voice so I backed off a little. "Look at you," I sneered. "Big war hero, sitting there drinking beer. Mama was right, you look just like the old man."

Donny's face reddened. For a minute I thought he was going to punch me, but he just sagged in on himself like an empty sack. "What do you expect, Gordo?" He paused to light another cigarette. "Don't forget, he's your old man too. You think you'll grow up to be the president or something?"

I backed off some more. "You dirty SOB," I yelled. "Why did you come back if this is how you're going to act?"

Donny swallowed a mouthful of beer and wiped his mouth with the back of his hand. How often had I seen the old man do the exact same thing? "Leave me be, Gordy." His voice was flat, empty. His eyes were dead.

"Go to hell," I said and ran around the house. This wasn't the Donny I'd expected. I didn't want to talk to him anymore, I didn't want to see him. He scared the living daylights out of me.

Things got worse instead of better. It seemed Donny was just set on making us miserable. He slept till noon every day, then sat around drinking beer and smoking all afternoon. At night he'd go places with a bunch of vets he'd met at a bar on Fourth Street. Mama fussed and worried about him, Grandma nagged him, but I stayed away from him. He wasn't a hero, he didn't have any medals, he was nobody to brag about. Just a bum, that's all he was. No better than the old man.

More than ever I missed William. If he'd been home I'd have talked to him about Donny. William would have figured out what was wrong with my brother. But days passed and William's house stayed empty. I began to think his mother was waiting for us to leave before she came home.

I started writing a long letter to Stu, thinking he might know what to say to pull Donny out of his bad mood, but my fingers started hurting and the paper stuck to my hand and I didn't know how to spell half the words I wanted to use. After tearing up five sheets of paper, I gave up. I couldn't seem to get my thoughts into writing.

One afternoon I got so desperate I tried talking to Grandma about Donny. "What do you think's wrong with him?" I asked her. "Why won't he talk to anybody?"

Grandma looked up from the apple she was paring. "Be patient with your brother, Gordon. He's been through a war. Seen things you and I can't even imagine."

"But he's home now. Why can't he just be his old self again?"

"It takes time," she said. "Donny has to heal."

"Huh," I snorted. "What do you mean, 'heal'? He wasn't wounded. He didn't even get a Purple Heart."

"It doesn't matter whether he was wounded or not. He has eyes, doesn't he? Ears?"

I picked up one of the long peels from the apple and curled it around my finger. It made a perfect red spiral, like blood from a cut. "If he doesn't watch out, he'll end up just like the old man," I muttered.

Grandma studied the apple as if she saw a worm in it. "I hope not," she said.

That was all she had to say on the subject. "I have a pie to bake," she said, getting to her feet. "Why don't you go outside and weed the garden? Pick some string beans for dinner, too."

I passed June on the way and took her along with me. After we'd weeded and filled a basket with beans, she and I sat down in the shade to rest.

"Daddy's coming soon," June said. "Mama told me."

"Is that supposed to make me happy?"

June shrugged. "Will he think I've grown, Gordy? Am I bigger now that I'm seven?"

Although I hadn't really noticed before, June was getting taller. Her legs were longer. The main difference, though, was in her smile and her eyes. She'd lost that pale, scared look that reminded me of kids in *Life* magazine pictures. Kids in the ruins of cities, kids getting treats from GIs, kids walking in long lines from one bombed place to another, kids with no homes, no parents, everything gone, nobody to protect them. DPs— displaced persons, they were called. Here at Grandma's, June had found a safe place.

"You're definitely bigger, June," I said, letting it go at that.

"You're bigger, too, Gordy."

"Yeah," I said, "I'm bigger."

June started giggling. "Bobby's bigger, Victor's bigger, Ernie's bigger, Donny's bigger, Mama's bigger, Grandma's bigger, the sky's bigger, the sun's bigger. Bigger, bigger, bigger—everything's bigger!"

By now the word *bigger* was just a silly sound; it didn't mean anything at all. I laughed too.

"Even Daddy." June giggled and stretched her arms toward the sky. "Daddy's bigger, bigger, biggest!"

I stopped laughing. "June, I know Mama's been telling you all kinds of stuff about California, but wouldn't you rather stay with Grandma? Don't you remember how it was when we lived with the old man? How scared you were?"

June folded her arms across her chest and hunched her shoulders. Without looking at me, she said, "Daddy's not like that now, Mama promised. She says he'll buy me a pony."

"Bull," I said. "That's bull, Junie. Mama's telling you stories."

"Why do you always have to ruin things, Gordy?" June's laughter turned to tears just as if somebody had thrown a switch. In a second, she was on her feet, running for the house as fast as she could go, pausing only long enough to scoop up the doll she'd left lying on the steps. Then she was gone. The screen door slammed shut like thunder behind her.

I sighed and rested my head against the tree trunk. In the dust at my feet, two ants were fighting over a crumb. I stepped on them both, but it didn't make me feel any better. A pony! Shoot. Why couldn't Mama fight fair?

Seventeen

✦ ✦ ✦ ✦ ✦ ✦

That night I went outside for some fresh air and found Donny sitting on the steps, smoking and staring into the dark. I thought he'd tell me to get lost, but he patted a place beside him and said, "Take a load off your feet, Gordo."

For a while we didn't talk. It wasn't any cooler outside than in, but it was kind of peaceful. The cicadas were making a din in the snowball bushes. Lightning bugs flickered all around, bright as stars. Way off on the horizon, heat lightning flashed, and every now and then thunder rumbled, too far away to worry about.

"So what do you think about the old man coming back?" Donny asked after a while. "Are you all excited about going to California?" His voice was sharp with sarcasm.

"Are you kidding?" I spat in the bushes. "I wouldn't go around the block with the old man. Not for a million bucks. How about you, Donny? Are you going with them?"

"I had enough of the old man when I was a kid," Donny said. "Besides, I start pumping gas at the Esso station next week. No sense going to California when I've got a job right here in Grandville."

He paused to light a cigarette. I was dying to ask him for one but I was scared of breaking the nice mood between us, so I just breathed in his smoke and pretended I had a Lucky Strike hanging from my lower lip too.

"Do you think Grandma will let me stay here?" I asked.

"Don't see why she wouldn't. So long as you behave yourself." Donny grinned. "That old bird doesn't take anything off anybody, does she?"

"I wish Mama was like Grandma," I said. "Maybe then she'd tell the old man to get lost and that would be the end of him."

"Sometimes I think Mama doesn't have good sense," Donny muttered. "Maybe the old man knocked her brains out once too often."

I'd been thinking that myself but it scared me to hear my brother say it. Made it true somehow. "She's better now than she was," I told him. "When we first got here, she wouldn't talk to anybody. Just sat around staring into space like she was shell-shocked or something."

"What do you know about shell shock?" Donny's voice was so low I almost didn't hear him.

"I read about it in *Life* magazine. Battle fatigue, they called it."

"Battle fatigue." Donny snorted. Suddenly he turned to me, his face so close I could smell beer and cigarettes on his breath. "You keep asking what the war was like. Do you really want to know?"

I nodded, but all of a sudden I wasn't so sure. "Are you drunk?"

Donny shrugged and took another swig of beer. "War is hell, just like some guy said a long time ago. Sherman, that's who said it, way back in the Civil War, I think."

I watched him swallow another mouthful of beer. "War's a lot of noise," he went on. "More noise than you ever heard in your whole entire life. It's men getting shot all around you. Screaming and dying in ways more horrible than you can imagine. It's never knowing when it'll be your turn to catch a bullet or step on a mine or get blown away by a shell. It's fires and ruins and death, Gordy. And stink, the worst stink you ever smelled. That's what war is."

Donny turned his head and looked me in the eye. "I'll tell you the truth, Gordy. If I'd known what I was getting into, I'd have hid in the woods like Stu. I swear to God it's what everybody should've done. The Krauts and the Japs included."

I didn't know what Donny expected me to say to that, so I kept quiet. It wouldn't do to tell him I was disappointed, maybe even a little bit sore to hear him talking like that. The way I saw it, Stu had always hated fighting, so it was natural for him to desert. But Donny was tough like me. He'd never run away from anybody.

"Most of us just wanted to stay alive," Donny said, more like he was talking to himself than to me. "Get out of there in one piece. Come home safe. Kill the Krauts before they killed us."

"But how about guys like Butch and Jimmy?" I asked, reminding him of guys we'd known back in College Hill. "They got medals. They were heroes." Heroes like I'd wanted Donny to be.

Donny put his head in his hands. "They died to get them, Gordo. That's why I'm here and they're not."

He paused to open another bottle of beer.

"There's this guy in my class named Jerry Langerman," I said while Donny fiddled with the opener. "His cousin won a bunch of medals but he didn't get killed getting them. He lets Langerman wear them to school."

"Bully for Langerman's cousin" was Donny's answer to that. "Bully for Langerman, too."

He sounded funny, kind of choked up. I couldn't tell if he was mad or not, so I just sat there, prying at a splinter on the top step. It was the kind that would really hurt if you stepped on it.

"Let me tell you about this guy in our outfit," Donny said after a while. "His name was Gerald and he was about thirty-five. Had a wife. Real pretty, I saw her picture. No kids, though, so he got drafted. From the day he joined our company, he was like a father to us.

Always joking about his age, saying he was too old for this, too old for that, but he always did it, whatever it was."

Donny took another swig of beer. "Gerald was a private like us, not an officer or anything, but he took care of us, Gordy, he looked out for us. He was the sweetest guy I ever met."

"What happened to him?" I thought I already knew.

"We were in France, somewhere near the German border, pushing hard. Killing Krauts. Getting killed. Living up to the great general's expectations. Good old Blood and Guts." Donny turned his head and spat on the ground to show me what he thought of General Patton.

"It was fall, late September, I think. The leaves were turning red, just like home." Donny glanced at me. "The woods were supposed to be clear, no Krauts, but all of a sudden a nest of machine gunners opened fire on us. Snipers hiding in the trees. We all hit the ground. A couple of guys were wounded, but nobody was killed."

I stared at my brother, but he was peering into the summer dark like he was seeing something altogether different from what I saw. Not the backyard squared with light from the kitchen windows. Not the fireflies in the bushes. Not the heat lightning. But a place he remembered. A place I'd never seen and never would. A bad place.

"Gerald's the first to see where the Nazis are," Donny went on. "'Stay low,' he tells us, 'I'll get them.' We're pinned down, Gordy, scared, but Gerald rises up real slow to throw a grenade."

Donny drank more beer. Even in the dark I could see how tightly he was holding the bottle. "The Krauts see him," he said. "They start firing. He's hit. We try to drag him back, but he's on his feet, throwing that grenade. Then he runs right at those German SOBs. Next thing he's killing the ones the grenade didn't finish. I never saw anything like it, Gordy. He wipes out the whole bunch and then, then—"

Donny hurled the empty beer bottle into the darkness. I heard the glass break. "Gerald died. He died right there with the Krauts. We had to leave him with them and go on."

He looked at me. "I'll never forget him lying there with those stinking Nazis. One American and six or seven Krauts. All dead."

There was no doubt about it. Donny was crying. Me, too. I'd never seen Gerald alive but I could imagine him lying there with the Nazis he'd killed. For some reason, I pictured a night scene with the moon shining down on the dead soldiers. Everything for miles around was torn up from bombs and shells and fighting. In the distance, the rest of Donny's squad was firing at the Nazis, but where Gerald lay everything was still and quiet like a scene in a play. Only no one was going to get up and take a bow at the end.

Donny wiped his eyes with the back of his hand. "Gerald saved the life of every guy in our squad, me included. He never thought of himself. Just us. The kids, he called us."

His voice shook and he paused to take a drag on his

cigarette. "I don't know how Gerald did that, Gordy, I really don't."

I waited for him to say something else, but he just sat there, smoking and thinking his own thoughts. Finally I said, "I'm sorry about Gerald, but I'm glad you didn't get killed, Donny. I'm glad you're here."

My brother put his arm around my shoulders and pulled me against his side. After a while, he said, "When I came home, you asked me about souvenirs. Well, I picked up a Nazi helmet for you, but I ended up throwing it away."

I told him it was okay, but I felt a little twinge of disappointment just the same. "Was it too heavy or something?"

"No, that wasn't it," he said. "Do you remember going to the beach once a long time ago? Way back before the war, when you were about three and Stu and me were in our teens? June wasn't even born yet."

I shook my head, surprised our family had ever done anything as nice as go to the beach. It was probably the only vacation we'd ever had. Didn't seem fair I'd been too little to remember it.

"We took the ferry across the bay and drove all the way to Ocean City," Donny said. "The old man was on the wagon, I guess, or we'd never have gone. Anyway, Stu found this seashell on the beach. One of those big ones you can hold up to your ear and hear the ocean."

I nodded. I'd seen those shells, but I couldn't figure out what they had to do with Nazi helmets.

"Well, he brought it back to the cabin where we

were staying and set it down by his bed," Donny went on. "The next night we started smelling this bad smell. I said maybe it was the old man's feet."

We both laughed because the old man's feet stunk so bad we used to hold our noses when he took off his shoes.

"Turned out this creature lived in the shell," Donny said. "Kind of like a snail or something. Anyway, it had died in there. We couldn't get the smell out so we threw the damn shell back in the ocean."

He looked at me. "That's how the helmet smelled, Gordy. Like something had died in it."

Donny flicked his cigarette butt into the yard. It glowed red for a second, then vanished in the dark. He kept his arm around my shoulders. I don't know how long we'd have sat there if a horn hadn't blown out front.

"That's the boys," Donny said, getting to his feet. "See you later, Gordo."

I followed him around the house and watched him get into an old Ford convertible with three or four other guys. The car radio was playing "Pistol-Packin' Mama," and I heard Donny start singing along with it, laughing with the others. Somebody yelled, "Yahoo!"

I waved, but Donny didn't look back. I guess he'd already forgotten me.

I stood there listening till the last sounds died away. Then I went inside. It seemed like my brother had told me a whole bunch of sad stories and then left me to take care of them while he went out drinking.

Eighteen

❖ ❖ ❖ ❖ ❖ ❖ ❖

L ater that night, I lay awake for a long time thinking about Gerald and what he'd done. Like Donny, I didn't understand how anybody could be that brave. To keep fighting even when you knew you were dying. That was something. For Gerald's sake, I hoped my brother would get himself together and do something good with his life.

But it didn't seem as if Donny was ready for that. Even after he started working at the Esso station, he went on drinking beer and hanging out at bars. Grandma kept saying, "Give him time, give him time," but finally she got tired of waiting and told him to shape up or ship out. And that's what he did. Found himself a room in a shabby old boarding house on Seventh Street and shipped out.

After Donny moved, I hung around the Esso station so much it's a wonder they didn't put me on the payroll too. I kept hoping we'd have some more talks like the one we'd had about Gerald, but Donny's boss made it clear he wasn't paying Donny to shoot the breeze with his kid brother. So we never got beyond sports and the war, which was dragging on like it would never end. I swear the Japs meant to fight till every one of them was dead and most of us as well.

One hot afternoon toward the end of July, June and I were picking Japanese beetles off Grandma's roses. They were tough little bugs with shiny green shells and brown wings, not quite as big as a dime, and they ate their way through everything if you let them. Even after you dropped them in a can of bug killer, they spun around on their backs as if they were trying to swim.

June hated the way the beetles buzzed and wiggled in her hand. She said the Japs must have sent them to America to ruin our crops, but I'd read somewhere that they came over here all by themselves in some bushes way before the war. No matter how often I told June this, she insisted she was right and I was wrong. When that kid believed something you couldn't get her to change her mind. She was that bullheaded.

"Did Mama tell you Daddy will be here either today or tomorrow?" June asked. Her face was scrunched up against the sun, squeezing her freckles together and making her eyes into little slits.

Before I answered, I dropped a beetle into my can and watched it die. The bug killer had a funny, sickly-sweet smell strong enough to make you sick, but that wasn't what made me feel like puking. Dumping more beetles into my can, I muttered, "Mama never tells me anything."

"That's because you're so hateful about Daddy," June said in the prissy little goody-goody voice she sometimes used.

"He's a hateful man," I said, struggling to keep my temper.

"You're just jealous because he's not bringing *you* a pony."

"He's not bringing you one either, June. I told you that's just one of Mama's crazy stories."

"Huh," said June. "You don't know everything, Mr. Smarty-Pants Gordy." Turning her back on me, she went on picking Japanese beetles off the roses. She was wearing a pink sunsuit Grandma had sewn for her. Under her bare skin, her shoulder blades wiggled like wings. Every time she dropped a bug in her can, she said, "Eeee-yoooo."

The old man didn't come that day or the next, but I swear I felt him getting closer and closer. We were all tense with waiting. Mama and Grandma got so edgy you couldn't say a word to either of them without starting an argument. The boys fussed and cried and fought with each other, driving us all crazy.

June spent hours hanging on the front gate, peering down the street as if she expected every car that turned the corner to be the old man's. She'd already named the pony Petunia and was planning to make a bed for it in Grandma's garage. Of course, she hadn't mentioned this to Grandma.

Three or four nights later, I was lying in bed, too hot to sleep. The temperature must have been close to ninety and I was wishing for a thunderstorm to break the heat wave.

Along about midnight I heard a car pass the house real slow. I lay still and waited for it to stop, but it went on by. A few minutes later it came back. I knew it was the same car because the muffler was bad. This time, it stopped out front.

Thinking it might be Donny, I went to the window to see what he was up to. Although the car was parked in the shadows under a tree, I recognized it. The old man had kept his promise. He was here.

I expected him to get out of the car and come to the house, but he just sat there smoking a cigarette. I could see the red tip glowing. I swear I even smelled the smoke mixed in with the sweet perfume of Grandma's roses.

The cicadas made their usual racket, a train blew for the crossing, a dog barked. The leaves hung still in the summer night. Nothing moved, nothing stirred either outside or in. Everything was ordinary except for one thing. The old man.

A few minutes passed. My heart beat loud and fast. The rest of me was as still as the old man, frozen, clenched tight as a fist. After a while, I started hoping he'd go away. Grandma had said he wouldn't have the nerve to come to her door. Maybe she was right.

Finally the old man threw his cigarette out of the car

window. It arced across the lawn and disappeared into the snowball bushes beside the front porch. At the same moment, I was startled to see Mama run as lightly as a girl across the moonlit lawn. She must have been waiting downstairs. I was sure she hadn't passed my door.

Without a word, she got into the car. Try as hard as I could, I wasn't able to see or hear what they said or did. After a long time, the driver's door opened and out stepped the old man, carrying a big suitcase. The moon shone full on his face as he walked around the car to open Mama's door. He didn't stagger or stumble. He was clean shaven, his hair was combed, his clothes were ironed. He'd even lost some weight. In fact, if I hadn't known better, I'd have thought he was just an ordinary guy, the kind of dad most kids have.

I watched Mama lead him up the sidewalk. He hesitated a moment at the bottom of the porch steps, and Mama whispered something to him. They came inside so quietly I wouldn't have heard them if I hadn't been listening for them.

Holding my breath, I slid into bed, closed my eyes, and lay still. I was afraid Mama might bring him into my room to say hello, but they passed by, tiptoeing and whispering to each other. Mama's door closed softly. I knew I was the only one besides Mama who knew the old man was in the house.

The next morning I told myself I'd dreamed the

whole thing. The old man couldn't be here. Not really. But when I went to the window to check, the car was right where I'd seen him park it. The shade of the trees dappled it like camouflage, but the sun shone on its windshield.

I pulled on my clothes slowly and dragged myself downstairs, hoping he was still sleeping. But before I got to the kitchen, I heard his voice.

"Why, just wait till you see California," he was saying. "It's like the Big Rock Candy Mountain. Lemons and oranges grow on the trees and the sun shines every day."

"And will I really have a pony?" June asked. She was sitting close to the old man, her eager eyes fixed on his face.

The old man grinned. "Sure, honey. A mockingbird, a diamond ring, a pony—Papa will buy his little girl anything her heart desires."

He looked up then and saw me in the doorway, staring knives and daggers at him.

"Why, Gordy," he said in the friendliest voice I had ever heard from him, "come here. Let me get a good look at you, son." He held out his hand as if he wanted me to shake it, but he didn't fool me. I stayed where I was.

Mama and June were watching me as if I was a bomb about to explode and wreck everything, but Bobby, Ernie, and Victor were too busy blowing on brand-new pinwheels to pay me any attention. I noticed June was holding one of those Shirley Temple dolls she'd always begged for. Mama was wearing a flowered sundress I'd never seen before. She'd slashed her mouth with bright red lipstick and painted her nails to match. I could smell her perfume from several feet away. Like the old man, she was playing at being somebody else.

Grandma stood at the sink, sipping a cup of coffee and looking out the window. She glanced over her shoulder at me, then turned her back on us again. She didn't have to say anything. I knew she was just as disgusted as I was.

June held the doll up. "See what Daddy brought me, Gordy? Isn't she pretty?" She smiled that hopeful smile, the one she'd used to good effect on Grandma.

"I brought something for you, too, Gordy." Like the ancient Greeks William had once told me about, the old man had come bearing gifts. Holding out his hand, he showed me mine—a pearl-handled penknife with a double blade, the kind I'd wanted all my life.

I stuck my hands in my pockets real fast because they were just itching to hold that knife. "Keep it," I muttered.

A frown slid across the old man's face so fast I was the only one to see it. "It's a good one," he said. "I paid a lot for it."

"I don't want it." I shoved my hands deeper into my pockets.

The old man shrugged and laid the knife on the kitchen table. It looked out of place among the coffee cups and cereal bowls and juice glasses. But, much as I wanted that knife, I didn't touch it. It could stay there forever. I wasn't taking anything from the old man— good or bad.

"Gordy's rude," said June. "Isn't he, Mama?"

Mama looked at me. Her eyes were flat and cold. "You could at least thank your father," she said. "You haven't even said hello to him. What's the matter with you?"

"Nothing."

Mama started to say more, but the old man cut her off. "Leave him be, Ginny. If he wants to bite off his nose to spite his face, it's okay by me." Turning to Bobby, he said, "Let me show you how that thing works, son."

Without touching my breakfast, I left the old man puffing on Bobby's pinwheel. Grandma had gone outside to weed the tomatoes but I didn't stop to talk to her. Hot as it was, I ran all the way to the Esso station to tell Donny the news.

I found him pumping gas into Dr. Langerman's big old fancy Buick. Mrs. Langerman was in the front seat, fanning her face with a magazine, and Langerman and his sisters were in the back. The girls were giggling over a comic book, but Langerman was sitting by a window, staring at the back of his mother's head like he was bored to death. Except for him, they looked like the perfect family, heading out to Long View Lake to have a picnic and wasting gas like the war was over.

I walked past the car and sneered at Langerman, but he pretended not to see me. I wished he was by himself. I felt like getting into a good fight.

Donny took Dr. Langerman's money and gas coupons before he turned to me. "What's up, Gordo?"

"Ten guesses," I said, giving Langerman the finger as the Buick sped off. "The first nine don't count."

Donny swore. "The old man's back."

"Got here last night. Brought everybody presents." I spit in the greasy dust by the pump.

"Drunk or sober?"

"Sober." I spit again. "For now."

"Wonder how long it'll last this time."

I shrugged and took a swig from the bottle of orange Nehi Donny handed me. The glass was cold and wet and so was the pop.

For a while we didn't talk, just leaned against the side of the garage, sharing the shade and the Nehi. We were brothers, Donny and me. We understood each other in a way nobody else could. Not even Stu. If he'd been here, he'd have wanted us to give the old man a chance. Donny and I knew better than to give the old man anything.

An Oldsmobile pulled up to the pump. The guy driving it blew his horn. "Hey, kid," he said, "are you going to hold that wall up all day or are you going to give me some gas?"

Donny handed me the Nehi and walked over to the car. I noticed he didn't hurry. After he'd filled the tank, washed the windshield, and checked the oil, he ambled back to the shade and squatted beside me.

"Someday I'll have a car like that," he said as the man drove away.

"Me, too," I said. "Only mine will have whitewall tires."

I hung around with Donny all day, cleaning windshields and checking oil, making change, breathing in the good smells of oil and grease and gasoline.

Around three, a familiar black car pulled into the gas station. The old man jumped out and slapped Donny on the back. "It's damn good to see you, son," he said, grinning from ear to ear.

Without giving Donny a chance to say a word, the old man started going on and on about how the army had made a man of him and crap like that. All the while the old man was talking, Mama sat in the car, holding Bobby and smiling that wounded red smile. In the back seat, June and Ernie and Victor were eating ice cream cones, licking them slowly, making them last. Just looking at them, anybody would have thought the Smiths were one big happy family, just like the Langermans.

I don't know how long the old man would've gone on talking about the war if Victor hadn't begun complaining about being hot.

"Hush up, Vic," he said. "Daddy hasn't forgotten. We're going to the park in just a minute."

Maybe it was my imagination, but I thought I heard a little edge creeping into the old man's voice. Maybe he was getting tired of playing his new part.

"Ernie keeps bumping my hand," Victor whined. "He's trying to make me drop my ice cream."

"I am not," Ernie said.

"You are too!" Victor punched Ernie. Ernie started to cry and hit Victor back.

"Don't fight, don't fight," June wailed, trying to separate her brothers. "You'll ruin everything!"

The old man muttered something under his breath and opened the car door. I held my breath when he got inside, but all he did was tell them to shut up.

"Got to go," he told Donny and me, gunning the motor.

Before the car pulled away, Mama called, "We're having a big dinner tonight in honor of your daddy. Five o'clock, boys. Don't be late, now."

Donny and I watched the car drive off. June and the little kids waved from the back window. Ernie was holding his pinwheel out to catch the breeze. It spun so fast you couldn't see the colors.

"Are you going to be there?" I asked Donny.

He lit a cigarette and exhaled smoke through his nose, a skill I hadn't yet managed, mainly due to lack of practice. "Only because I don't want to hurt Mama's feelings," he muttered. "The old man will do that soon enough."

I knew what he meant. Mama was desperate to believe the old man was on the level this time. Naturally she wanted us kids to be as happy as she was. But that wasn't possible for Donny and me. Neither one of us was about to forget the stuff the old man had done. We had plenty of scars to remind us.

Like Donny, I figured I'd show up for dinner, too. I didn't want to hurt Mama's feelings any more than he did. Nor did I want to miss seeing how Grandma planned to handle the welcome home party. Somehow I couldn't picture her festooning the dining room with crepe paper streamers and fixing the old man's favorite meal, whatever that might be.

Nineteen

❖ ❖ ❖ ❖ ❖ ❖ ❖

I went over to Donny's room after he got off work and waited for him to take a shower and change. It wasn't much of a place to live, I thought. Stifling hot and barely big enough for a bed, a chest of drawers, a little table for his radio, and a shabby armchair. One window propped open with a stick. Cinders half an inch deep on the sill. Dingy lace curtains framing a view of a lumberyard and the railroad tracks. No doubt the bed shook when a train passed, just like it had in College Hill.

Donny left the radio playing for me, one of those corny wartime songs about walking alone and feeling lonely. I don't know if it was the words of the song or the faded wallpaper or the saggy old chair, but something about the setup made me sad. Donny had fought his way across Europe and this was all he'd come home to. Of course it was better than a grave in Europe or Okinawa or some other foreign place, but it didn't seem fair. After all they'd gone through, it seemed to me soldiers deserved better. But that was just my opinion. What did I know?

Donny came back from his shower looking clean and fresh. "You better wash up too," he said, tossing me the soap and a towel. "The shower's down the hall on the left."

"What's the use? I don't have any clean clothes to change into." Glad to have an excuse, I threw the soap and towel back. I never took showers unless somebody like Grandma made me.

Donny shrugged. "Have it your way, Gordo. Don't blame me, though, if nobody wants to sit next to you."

I laughed and punched his arm and he punched me back. Not hard. Just in fun.

By the time we'd walked the eight blocks to Grandma's house, the whole family was sitting at the table waiting for us. The old man frowned and glanced at his watch. Donny mumbled something about his job and took a seat next to Ernie. I dropped into a chair across the table from him. Grandma sat at the head, the old man faced her at the other end, with Mama on his right and June on his left.

"Everybody's here but Stu," the old man said, looking up and down the table as if what he saw pleased him. "We sure don't miss *him*, do we?"

I wasn't sure who he was talking to. Neither was anyone else because nobody said anything.

"Never thought a son of mine would turn out to be a coward," the old man went on. "Did everything I could to make a man of him. Nothing worked. Why, June here's got more backbone than Stu ever had."

Still nobody said a word. Mama took a sip of iced tea. Grandma buttered a roll. June fidgeted. The little boys ate without looking up. Donny cleared his throat but kept silent otherwise.

"You know what I hope?" The old man's voice rose as if he thought nobody was listening. "I hope the army puts him away for life. I hope they throw the book at him."

"They might as well," Donny said quietly. "You threw just about everything else at him."

"What did you say?" The old man leaned toward Donny.

Mama cast Donny a begging look and he shook his head. "Nothing," he muttered.

The old man nodded as if he'd decided to accept that. "You served," he said. "You did your share, you answered your country's call. You've got nothing to be ashamed of, son."

When Donny didn't answer, the old man said a few more patriotic things. Finally he gave up and let us eat in peace.

I don't know why, but Grandma had gone all out to fix a great meal. Pot roast, mashed potatoes and gravy, corn and beans from the garden. Fresh-baked rolls and coleslaw, too. Maybe she thought she had a duty to make Mama happy. Or maybe she thought we wouldn't be getting any more good dinners if we went off with the old man.

About halfway through the meal, the old man lit a cigarette. Grandma looked at him and said, "Please don't smoke at the table, Roger."

He narrowed his eyes and laid the cigarette on the edge of his plate. Didn't put it out, just left it there. The smoke drifted past June. She made a face and tried to wave it away with her hand.

"Roger," Grandma said, still calm, still reasonable, "you can go outside and smoke after dinner. That's what Virginia does."

The old man just looked at her. Though I'd seen it before, I didn't like the expression on his face.

Mama shot a frown at Grandma and then touched the old man's hand the way you might touch a bear or a wolf. "Mother doesn't allow smoking in the house, Roger. I told you. Don't you remember, honey?" Her voice had a sickening sweetness that riled me.

"I always smoke at dinner," said the old man. To prove it, he picked up the cigarette and took a drag so deep I could almost feel it burn the back of my throat.

Grandma got up and left the room. I was amazed at her for giving in so quick, but I should have known better. In a few seconds she was back, carrying a pan of water. Before the old man knew what she was doing, she grabbed the cigarette and dropped it into the water. The room was so quiet we all heard the hiss it made.

The old man's face reddened. "Why, you old son of a—" Somehow he stopped himself. "You wasted a perfectly good cigarette. Do you know how hard it is to get ahold of a Camel these days?"

Grandma didn't bother to answer. She walked into the kitchen, opened the screen door, and flung the water into the backyard, cigarette and all. Then, without even looking at the old man, she sat back down. "Would anyone care for more mashed potatoes?" she asked. "They're getting cold."

I heard the old man swear under his breath. He was fighting to keep his evil self from breaking loose, I had to give him credit for that. But I was braced for an explosion.

June must have sensed trouble coming too. Thinking she could ward it off, she smiled her bright puppy-dog smile and nudged the old man. "Look, Daddy, Shirley can do a trick." Holding her new doll by its arms, she spun its body. "See? She does somersaults."

Unfortunately, the doll's feet hit the old man's glass of iced tea. Over it went, pouring into his lap like Niagara Falls. Before June knew what was happening, he'd cracked her on the head with his knuckles. I'd gotten plenty of those knuckle raps. I knew how much they hurt, especially if you weren't expecting it.

"Can't you be more careful or are you just naturally clumsy?" the old man shouted.

June started crying and jumped up from the table. The old man grabbed her arm. "Sit down and behave yourself! You can leave when I say so. Not before!"

June cried harder.

"Stop that bawling," the old man said, "or I'll give you something to cry about."

Grandma got to her feet and pulled June away from him. "That's enough, Roger. There's no need to carry on like this. The child didn't mean to knock over your tea."

"She's my daughter," the old man yelled, grabbing June back. "I'll punish her as I see fit. Don't you interfere!"

Caught between them, June wailed hysterically. Bobby began to cry. So did Ernie. Victor just sat there with his thumb in his mouth, staring. Mama hid her face in her hands. Donny threw his napkin down and swore at the old man. It was a familiar scene—The Smiths' Dinner Hour, brought to you tonight by Camel cigarettes, preferred by doctors everywhere.

With one difference. Instead of hitting Donny, the old man cursed and strode out of the room. The back door slammed behind him.

Mama raised her head and glared at Grandma. "I hope you're satisfied, Mother."

With that, she threw her napkin on the table and hurried after the old man. The door slammed again. My three little brothers ran after her. *Bang, bang, bang* went the screen door.

While Grandma tried to comfort June, Donny and I looked at each other.

"So, what's new?" Donny asked and walked out the front door.

I ran after him but he turned me back at the gate.

"I'm going to Malone's," he said. "I told the guys I'd meet them there."

I grabbed his arm. "Can I come with you? I swear I won't say anything, you won't even know I'm there, I won't ask you for a Coke, I won't ask for anything at all, I'll just sit there. Let me come, Donny, just let me."

Donny lit a cigarette and squinted at me through the smoke. "You got years ahead of you to hang out in bars if that's what you want to do with your life," he said. "There's no sense starting now, Gordo."

I thought about arguing, I thought about following him, but I knew it wouldn't do any good. I'd just make him mad.

So I stood at the gate and watched Donny walk into the summer evening, slump-shouldered. The sun was low in the sky behind him, and his shadow stretched ahead as if it was leading the way and he was following.

When Donny turned the corner at the end of the block, I swung back and forth on the gate for a while, listening to it squeak. The windows in William's house reflected the sunset as if lights shone in all the rooms, but I knew no one was home. Grandma had told me Mrs. Sullivan planned to stay away all summer. It was cooler at her sister's place, she claimed, better for William. Anything was better for William than I was.

I swung faster, wishing I'd look up and see him sitting on the front porch, waiting for me to come over. I sure would have liked to talk to him.

"William," I'd say, "I know this is a terrible thing to

say, but it should've been my old man who got killed in the war instead of your father."

"Get off that gate, Gordon," Grandma called from the front porch. "You'll break it."

I felt like mouthing off to her, that was the kind of terrible mood I was in, but I ran off down the sidewalk instead. I heard her calling me back, but I kept going. Nobody liked me, nobody wanted me, nobody cared what happened to me. Not Grandma, not Mama, not Donny. I was all alone in the world.

Such thoughts would have made a kid like William cry, but not me. I was as tough and mean as they come. Nothing made Gordy Smith cry. Not even the worst beating the old man could give me.

Twenty

❖ ❖ ❖ ❖ ❖ ❖ ❖ ❖

I walked around town for a couple of hours, looking for something to do. Nobody was around. Not Langerman or any of his buddies. I had to content myself writing cuss words on the school sidewalk with a piece of soft rock that rubbed off like red chalk on the cement. I'd have broken some school windows if Mrs. Maxwell hadn't been sitting on her front porch, watching me.

By the time I dragged myself home, it was dark. The night was steamy hot. Heat lightning flickered, lighting the sky like flares, and thunder rumbled softly like a tiger growling somewhere far off. The air seemed as if it wanted to rain but couldn't quite find the energy to do it.

Mama and the old man were sitting in the porch swing. June perched on the old man's knee, smiling as if she'd already forgotten getting a knuckle rap. Mama cuddled Bobby, and Ernie and Victor ran around the yard chasing fireflies. The only person missing from the happy family scene was Grandma.

"Where have you been, Gordy?" the old man barked from the shadows.

"Nowhere." Without waiting to see what he'd say next, I went inside and let the screen door slam good and hard behind me. The old man might fool the others, but not me. I was too smart for him.

I found Grandma sitting on the back steps. She didn't say anything when I dropped down beside her.

"Looks like everything's peachy-keen now," I muttered.

I knew Grandma knew what I meant, but instead of saying anything about the old man, she murmured, "I wish it would rain. Everything in the garden is doing poorly except the weeds. Why do they thrive when nothing else does?"

It seemed to me that was the way it went. Good things died, bad things lived. And not just in gardens, either. But I had other stuff on my mind, important stuff I wanted to talk about.

"What's wrong with Mama?" I asked. "Why is she so dumb about the old man? You know how he used to treat her, don't you?"

Grandma didn't answer right away. For a minute, I thought she was going to tell me such things were none of my business. A lot of grown-ups would have. But Grandma wasn't like most people. "Virginia told me a lot before she brought you all down here," she said at last. "Then, after Roger started writing to her, she clammed up again."

She shook her head slowly. "My only child," she murmured, "and we can't be in the same room for five minutes without quarreling. I don't understand her. She's a stranger to me." Grandma sounded about as sad as a person can sound.

"Did Mama tell you he broke her arm once?" I asked. "Gave her black eyes? Knocked out a tooth?"

Grandma nodded. "She claims he's changed."

"Sure he has." I spit as far as I could into the dark. "You saw how he acted at dinner."

"Maybe I shouldn't have antagonized him," Grandma said.

"Baloney." I spit again, harder this time. "He was just showing a little bit of his true self. He can't hide it for long, you know. Especially if he starts drinking."

"I haven't seen any sign of alcohol," Grandma said. "Maybe he really is trying, Gordon. Maybe we should give him a chance."

"You're just as dumb as Mama if you believe that," I said, daring her to get mad at me.

Grandma sighed and got to her feet. "I'm going to bed now, Gordon. Don't stay up too late."

After she went inside, I sat on the steps watching the heat lightning snake back and forth, leaping from cloud to cloud like fires burning in heaven. I wondered if that was how the sky looked at night during a battle. Shells exploding, bombs falling, flares lighting up the ground. And all the time the rumble and roar of guns louder than thunder. Guys like Gerald dying. Guys like Donny crouching in foxholes, scared to raise their heads.

A burst of laughter from the front porch reminded

me of the old man sitting in the swing with Mama just like he belonged there. Grandma had said she hadn't seen any signs of alcohol, but what if she'd missed something? I knew where to look, I knew his secret places.

My eyes moved to the black car sitting in the driveway. The old man used to keep a pint of Lord Calvert in the glove compartment and a couple more under the seat. I knew because Donny had bragged about stealing a bottle for a last bash with his buddies before he went off to basic training.

Careful to stay in the shadows, I sneaked around the side of the house to see what was going on. Just as I'd thought, the old man and Mama were still sitting in the swing.

Bobby had fallen asleep in Mama's lap, but June, Victor, and Ernie were playing statues on the lawn. June swung the boys round and round by their arms, calling out to Mama and the old man every time one of her brothers fell into a new pose. "Guess what Victor is! Guess what Ernie is!"

Spinning herself around till she fell, she cried, "Look, look! Guess what I am!"

Mama and the old man ignored her, but she kept on trying to get their attention anyway.

Thinking I was safe, I ran to the car and opened the door real quietly. The dome light went on but I figured nobody'd see it. First I searched the glove compartment. Out tumbled gas-ration books, maps, a pack of Camels, a snapshot of Mama taken on a long-ago, smiling day at the beach, matchbooks from different places between here and California. But no whiskey.

I put the Camels in my pocket and looked under the front seat. Nothing there. Was I disappointed or relieved? I didn't know, so I kept on searching.

I was just about to open the trunk when somebody grabbed my arm.

"What the hell are you doing, Gordy?"

It was the old man.

I pulled free and backed away, stumbling on loose stones. He didn't come any closer. A flash of lightning lit his face but it didn't show his eyes.

"There's no bottle in the car," he said, "if that's what you're thinking."

"You must have hidden it someplace else, then."

"I told you I've quit drinking."

"I've heard that before."

The old man reached out and grabbed my jersey, yanking me closer. "Ginny's right," he muttered. "Your grandmother's turned you kids against me. Brainwashed you."

He started cussing Grandma, calling her names, blaming everything on her. She'd always hated him. Now she'd made us kids hate him too. Nobody liked him in this town, never had, never would. He shouldn't have come back, he should've stayed in California.

"Grandma's got nothing to do with how I feel about you," I shouted. "I hate you because of what you've done, not because of anything she's said."

The old man tightened his grip on my jersey, twisting the neck so it nearly choked me. "Don't sass me, you little SOB," he said, cuffing one side of my face and then the other. "I'm your father, goddammit! Show me some respect!"

Before he could hit me again, the back porch light flashed on, flooding the driveway and the yard beyond. "What's going on out there?" Grandma called.

The old man let me go with a curse. Dizzy from the blows he'd landed, blood spurting out of my nose, I ran past Grandma and pounded up the stairs to my room. Slamming the door shut, I shoved my bureau in front of it and waited for the old man to come banging on the door, threatening and cursing me.

Let him try it, just let him. He'd see I wasn't a little kid. He couldn't beat me the way he used to. Not anymore.

Twenty-one

❖ ❖ ❖ ❖ ❖

After fifteen or twenty minutes, I decided the old man wasn't coming, but I left the bureau where it was just in case. My heart slowed down to normal and my nose stopped bleeding, but I still felt pretty edgy. To calm my nerves, I lit one of the Camels I'd stolen from the car and sat in the dark, blowing the smoke out the window so Grandma wouldn't smell it.

I hadn't smoked for a long time and it made me feel kind of sick and dizzy, but I didn't want to waste a cigarette. Once you lit one you had to finish it. That's what Donny told me when he taught me to smoke.

Besides, smoking helped me think. There was no way on earth I was going to California or anywhere else with the old man. As much as I longed to see that redwood forest, I'd find some other way to get across the country.

For now, I wanted to stay right here at Grandma's house. She was strict and sometimes as cross as an old maid schoolteacher, but she never hit me or yelled at me or cussed me out. Never called me stupid, either. She fed me three meals a day—not just something from a can but good stuff. Best of all, I could fall asleep at night without being scared of what might happen before the sun came up the next day.

The trouble was, I didn't know if Grandma wanted me. It was true we got along better than we used to, but she never kissed me the way she kissed June and the little boys, never hugged me or called me honey. Not that I wanted her mushing over me or anything. But I was still Gordon to her, for Pete's sake, not even Gordy.

While I thought about all this, I smoked my cigarette right down to the end and ground it out in a little china dish on my night table. I hid everything—the cigarettes and the dish—in the bottom drawer of my bureau. I didn't want Grandma to find the Camels. If she knew I smoked, she definitely wouldn't want me living in her house.

I lay down on my bed but it was too hot to sleep. I'd read all the Hardy Boys mysteries William had loaned me and every Captain Hornblower story in the old *Saturday Evening Posts* I'd brought upstairs. I'd even tackled a few of Grandma's books, like *Around the World in Eighty Days* and *The Adventures of Sherlock Holmes*, which were longer and harder than anything I'd ever read. But I kept going, skipping words I didn't understand and long, boring descriptions, because I wanted to know what happened next. I also had an idea I'd impress William when he came back by telling him how much I'd read.

Now all that was left in the bookcase was *Heidi* and some other girl books from Mama's childhood. I wasn't about to read them.

So I lay there, hot and sweaty, staring at the ceiling with no way to escape from my own thoughts, till a noise at the door made me sit up and take notice.

"Who's there?" I whispered, scared it was the old man coming after me just when I'd thought I was safe.

"It's me," June whispered. "Let me in, Gordy."

I shoved the bureau aside and opened the door. June ran into the room and jumped on my bed. In the dim light, her face was nothing but a pale oval, but I could tell she'd been crying.

I sat down beside her. "What's wrong?"

"It's Daddy," she whimpered. "He told me I was a show-off trying to hog everybody's attention. Then I heard him tell Mama I looked just like Grandma. He said I was all Aitcheson."

She barely got the last words out before she started crying again. "And I've been trying so hard to be good, Gordy. I didn't mean to spill the tea, I didn't mean to make him mad, I just wanted him to love me, but he doesn't, he doesn't love me at all."

"Oh, Junie." I patted her skinny little shoulder, hating the old man even more for making her so unhappy. "It's not your fault," I muttered. "He's always been mean. You just forgot, that's all."

When June calmed down some, I got another cigarette and lit it.

June drew in her breath. I thought she was shocked to see me smoking but it was my eye that upset her. She must have seen my face in the flare of the match. "Did Daddy hit you?"

I touched my eye, feeling the old, familiar stab of pain. "What do you think?"

June took another deep gulping breath. "I don't want to go with Daddy. Not even if he gives me a pony. I want to stay with Grandma."

"She'd love that," I said, trying not to sound jealous.

"Do you really think so?"

"Grandma's crazy about you," I said, "probably because you're all Aitcheson." To make it sound like a little joke, I laughed. Unfortunately, I'd just taken a deep drag on my cigarette and I practically coughed a lung out. Boy oh boy, that's how out of practice I was.

"How about you, Gordy?" June asked. "Are you staying with Grandma too?"

"I doubt she wants me," I said. "Maybe Donny will take me in. If not, I'll go back to College Hill and live in the woods. It can't be more than five or six hundred miles from here."

June didn't say anything. When I looked at her, I saw she'd fallen asleep, thumb in her mouth, taking up almost the entire bed. I finished my cigarette and curled up in the space she'd left.

When I woke up, June was gone. I dressed and went downstairs. The old man was sitting at the kitchen table, drinking a cup of coffee. Mama perched on a chair beside him. Her suitcase and several bags of stuff sat by the door. Nobody said a word about my eye, which was puffed nearly shut. I doubt Mama even noticed.

"Get your things packed, Gordy," the old man said, "and tell June to get a move on, too. I sent her upstairs half an hour ago."

I looked at Mama. "Where's Grandma?"

Mama shrugged. "Out back, weeding the garden or something."

The old man glanced at his watch. "I want to leave at ten," he said. "That gives you fifteen minutes to get ready, Gordy."

I folded my arms across my chest and said, "I'm not going with you."

In the sudden silence, I heard my brothers playing war in the backyard. "*Ackety-ackety-ack,*" Victor shouted. "You're dead, Ernie!"

The old man stared at me as if he'd never seen me before. "What are you talking about, you little snot?"

I took a step backward and nearly bumped into June. She'd come up behind me so quietly I hadn't heard her. "I'm staying here," I said. "So's June."

"The hell you are."

I took another step backward. Getting to his feet, the old man came toward me, his fist raised.

"Don't hit Gordy again!" June hollered, throwing herself between the old man and me. "Don't you dare!"

At the same moment, the screen door opened and Grandma stepped into the kitchen. She took in the scene like someone arriving late for a play and trying to figure out what was going on.

"No one will be hit in my house," she said firmly, never taking her eyes off the old man.

He shrugged and picked up his coffee cup. "I don't know what you're talking about," he muttered. "I'm just trying to get these kids packed and ready to go."

"We're not going with you!" June and I yelled together, as if we'd rehearsed our lines.

Grandma put her arm around June. "You can leave the children here if you want to," she told the old man.

I waited to see if Grandma would put her other arm around me. When she didn't, I moved several feet away and leaned against the wall. She wanted June, not me. I didn't care. I had other plans anyway— Donny, College Hill, maybe even Stu.

The old man started yelling then. We were his kids, he said. Grandma was an interfering old busybody, she'd turned us against him. He wouldn't let her keep us, no, siree. He'd take her to court, he'd sue her for every cent she had, she'd die penniless in the gutter.

While the old man ranted and raved, Mama sat at the table like a zombie. No expression on her face. Saying nothing. Not even looking at anybody till Bobby came running inside and climbed onto her lap.

No one else said anything, either. Not even Grandma. We just rode out the storm, waiting for the old man to run out of steam.

When he finally stopped shouting, Grandma said,

"Listen to me, Roger. I'm offering to help. Go back to California, take Virginia if she insists, but leave the children here. You can send for them later, when you're settled."

The old man started to argue but something stopped him. He eyed June and me as if he was calculating what it would cost to feed us and clothe us and take care of us. Pouring himself another cup of coffee, he went to the screen door and stood there with his back to us, drinking the coffee and staring at the yard.

I looked at Mama, expecting her to say something. After all, we were her children, too. Didn't she care what happened to us? But she looked as confused as the rest of us.

June edged away from Grandma and slipped her hand into mine. It felt boneless, tiny, easy to hurt.

We waited for the old man to finish his coffee. I thought he might turn around and throw the cup at Grandma. Or pick up a chair and hurl it out the door. Kick a hole in the wall. Beat me.

Finally he said, "If any of you kids stay here, I never want to see you again. I disown you. You will be dead to me." He kept his back turned while he spoke.

That was fine with me. It was exactly what I wanted. But June whimpered as if she might change her mind and run to the old man. I tightened my hand around hers, keeping her with me.

Still without looking at any of us, the old man opened the kitchen door and stepped outside. "I'll be waiting in the car," he said. "Ten minutes. Then I'm gone."

The door slammed shut behind him, and Mama got to her feet, still holding Bobby.

"Think carefully, Virginia," Grandma said. "If you go with that man, I won't take you back."

"Don't worry," Mama said coldly. "I'll never set foot in this house again."

June started to cry. "Don't go with Daddy, Mama. Stay here. Please, Mama, please."

Mama turned to Grandma, her face dark with anger. "See why I'm leaving? You've turned my own daughter against me."

"You think I'm responsible?" Grandma grabbed my shoulders and whirled me around to face Mama. "For God's sake, Virginia, look at your son. Look at his eye. How can you think about leaving here with a man who'd do something like this to his own son?"

Mama held Bobby tighter. "Gordy asked for it," she said. "Roger caught him looking for whiskey in the car. A boy like that belongs in reform school!"

"You don't believe that, Virginia," Grandma said, letting me go.

"You wait," Mama said. "Gordy's rotten to the bone. Whipping's the only way to make him behave. You'll see."

Grandma swore, which shocked me even more than Mama's opinion of me, but Mama paid no attention. She was done with us. Without looking at me, she went to the door and called Victor and Ernie. "Come get your bags, boys. We're leaving now."

When my little brothers came into the kitchen,

Grandma drew them close for good-bye kisses, but they pulled away, anxious to please Mama. I wanted to warn them about so many things, but there wasn't time. Instead I watched them stagger down the steps with their bags and hurry to the old man waiting in the car.

I thought Mama might say good-bye to me or at least wave, but she didn't. The last I saw of her was her back disappearing into that black car. She was still wearing the flowered sundress the old man had given her. The bottom of the skirt hung below the car door after she closed it. By the time she noticed, the dress would be ruined.

As the car backed out of the driveway, June broke away from me and ran after it, crying and calling out to Mama. "Wait, wait, I changed my mind," she screamed. "I want to go with you. Don't leave me, Mama, don't leave me!"

If Mama or the old man heard my sister, they gave no sign. The car picked up speed and vanished. Long after it was out of sight, the sound of its bad muffler echoed in my head.

Twenty-two

❖   ❖   ❖   ❖   ❖

"What now?" I asked Grandma, feeling more uneasy than I wanted to admit.

Instead of answering, Grandma opened her arms to comfort June. "It's all right, honey, it's all right," she murmured over and over again, patting her hair and shoulders, trying to calm her.

But it wasn't all right. Grandma knew it, June knew it, I knew it. Our mother had gone off with the old man. Who hadn't changed. And never would. Drunk or sober, he'd shown us his true self over and over again. Worse yet, Mama had taken three poor little kids with her.

When June had cried herself into dry sobs, Grandma led her upstairs, with me following close behind. From the door, I watched Grandma settle June on her bed and then sit down beside her.

"You rest, darling," she murmured. "Things will look better when you wake up, I promise they will."

While Grandma sang a soothing song to June, I went to my room. It was pretty clear she didn't want me. As I dumped my stuff out of the bureau drawers, I reminded myself I didn't care. Donny'd take me in. Maybe I wouldn't live right next door to William, but I'd still be able to come see him when he came back. And June, too.

"What are you doing, Gordon?" Grandma suddenly appeared in the doorway, hands on her hips, staring at me.

"What's it look like?" I made my voice ugly so she'd know I didn't care whether she wanted me or not.

Grandma studied the paper bags packed with my belongings. "It looks like you're planning on leaving."

"What if I am?" I narrowed my good eye to a slit and gave her my best Humphrey Bogart sneer. "I'm sure you'll be glad to get rid of me."

Grandma folded her arms across her chest. "You do beat everything, Gordon."

It seemed to me she was trying not to laugh but I figured I must be wrong. Nobody laughed at me. Not when I was looking my meanest.

Before I could think of a good comeback, Grandma said, "Didn't I tell your mother you could stay with me?"

"I figured you meant June, your *darling*, your *honey*." I spit out the last words, hating the sound of them.

"Did I say that?" Grandma asked. "Did I limit the offer to your sister?"

The old lady had me there. "No," I muttered, "but—"

Grandma interrupted me. "Have you ever known me to say anything I didn't mean?"

"No, ma'am," I admitted, feeling a little surge of hope run through my veins. "I have never heard you speak anything but the truth."

"Well, then." Grandma picked up my bags and emptied them onto my bed. "Put your things away," she said. "And make your bed. You're staying right here."

Grandma looked as if she expected me to argue, but I had a strange urge to throw my arms around her and hug her, maybe even kiss her. Instead, I started putting my underwear back in the bureau, working fast, hoping she wouldn't see the pack of Camels.

While I worked, Grandma paced around my room, finally coming to a stop by the window. She fiddled with the cord on the blind, running it up and down a few times as if she was testing it. Finally she spoke. "I don't know where your grandfather and I went wrong, but we surely missed the boat with Virginia. Now it seems the good Lord has given me a second chance at raising children. I mean to do it right this time, Gordon."

No doubt Grandma meant June and I were going to behave ourselves. Me especially. And not just at home. If I knew Grandma, I'd have to behave in school, too. And anywhere else I might go in Grandville.

Suddenly Grandma reached into the drawer I'd just filled with shirts and pulled out the pack of Camels. "I won't tolerate smoking," she said.

I gawked at Grandma, too surprised to argue. For an old lady, she sure had sharp eyes. Either that or I wasn't as quick as I thought.

"Did you steal these?" she asked. "I know you didn't have the money to buy them."

I felt my cheeks turn red. "I found them in the old man's car when I was hunting for whiskey. And not to drink, either," I added quickly, in case she believed what Mama had said. "He used to keep a pint in the glove compartment and another couple under the seat. I was just checking to see if he'd really quit, that's all."

Grandma gave me a long measuring look that said more than words ever could. "If I thought you intended to drink it," she said, "I'd send you off to reform school so fast your head would spin."

Suddenly she smiled a big smile, the first one she'd ever aimed at me. "Oh, don't look so mean, Gordy. You aren't nearly as bad as you'd like people to think you are."

I ducked away, embarrassed but kind of pleased, too. After all this time, she'd finally called me Gordy.

"Soon it'll be time for lunch," Grandma said. "Come on downstairs. I'll fix you a peanut butter and jelly sandwich and a glass of chocolate milk."

Just as June and I were finishing the cookies Grandma had given us for dessert, Donny showed up, looking down in the mouth as usual. Maybe he had a hangover, maybe he'd had a bad night. Maybe it was just life in general. With Donny you couldn't tell.

"What's so important you couldn't say it over the phone?" he asked Grandma. "I have to be at work in half an hour."

"Daddy and Mommy left," June said through a mouthful of cookie. "They took Victor and Ernie and Bobby. Now I guess they'll have the pony, not me."

June had gotten over the worst of her crying but she was still upset about the stupid pony. I'd told her the old man was lying. There'd never be a pony. Not for her. Not for her brothers either. But for some reason she couldn't let go of the idea that she'd been cheated out of something.

Donny stared at June and then turned to Grandma. "What's she talking about?"

"It's true," Grandma said. "Your mother and father left this morning after one big hullabaloo. It's a wonder you didn't hear it all the way over on Seventh Street. They took the three little ones, but Gordon and June refused to go."

Donny touched my eye gently and scowled at Grandma. "Look at that," he said. "The old man hasn't changed. Why the hell did Mama go with him?"

"Virginia's a fool," Grandma said, not caring she was insulting our mother.

"The hell with both of them," Donny said, "and the damn pony, too."

I laughed but June started bawling. That pony was no joke to her.

"Watch your mouth, Donald," Grandma said, but she gave him a cup of coffee anyway.

Just as Donny got to his feet to leave, something on the radio caught his attention. "Hush," he said, turning up the volume.

The four of us gathered close to hear the biggest news since V-E Day. The United States dropped an atom bomb on Hiroshima. The announcer claimed it was the most powerful bomb ever made. Nothing like it had been used before. "We've unleashed the power of the universe," he said in a hushed voice.

Giving a loud whoop, Donny picked up June and waltzed her around the kitchen. "This is it, June Bug," he shouted. "The war will be over soon, just you wait and see!"

June hugged Donny, her eyes wide. No wonder she looked confused. The war had been going on longer than she could remember.

The only quiet one was Grandma. She stood still, her hands pressed to her heart, and gazed out the window at the blue sky. "Oh, Lord," she whispered, "a bomb the equal of twenty thousand tons of TNT. What have we done?"

Donny and I stopped yelling and stared at her. "What's wrong?" I asked. "Aren't you glad?"

Grandma pinched her lips together as if she was trying to keep someone from giving her a spoonful of poison. "So much destruction," she said. "Think of the innocent people. Children, babies . . ."

"Innocent people?" Donny frowned. "You think those

Japs are innocent? Who started all this, Grandma? Who bombed Pearl Harbor? They deserve everything we do to them."

"It wasn't the children who bombed Pearl Harbor," Grandma said. "It wasn't the women and the old people."

"Grandma, we have to stop the war," Donny said. "Do you want more soldiers to get killed invading Japan? Haven't enough died already?" Donny's voice cracked and he turned away, reaching for his cigarettes.

"Just pray no one drops an atom bomb on this country," Grandma said before she went outside to pick beans for supper.

That would never happen, I thought, but June followed Grandma, looking worried. "Does Hitler have an A-bomb, too?" I heard her ask. Poor kid, she'd been scared of Hitler so long she couldn't believe he was really dead.

"Look at the time," Donny said suddenly. "I've got to get to work. I don't want Manny yelling at me for being late."

I tagged along behind my brother, but he stopped me at the gate. "Where do you think you're going, runt?"

"With you," I said, hoping to share an orange Nehi and shoot the breeze with the guys.

Donny shook his head. "No, siree. Manny's getting tired of seeing you following me from pump to pump, begging gum and soda pop. You don't want to get me fired, do you?"

"We just dropped the atom bomb, Donny. Nobody's going to care if you're late or if I'm with you. In fact, I bet good old Manny closes the station."

"I said no." Without looking at me again, Donny left, lighting a cigarette as he walked away.

I hung on the gate, swinging back and forth, watching my brother's back till he turned the corner. It seemed our family was getting smaller and smaller. Stu gone. Mama and the old man on their way to California with my little brothers. Donny living over on Seventh Street, drifting further and further away every day.

June was all I had now. And Grandma—who was going to yell at me for swinging on the gate if I wasn't careful.

Twenty-three

❖ ❖ ❖ ❖ ❖

Two days later we gave Tojo another dose of the atom bomb. This time we hit Nagasaki. President Truman said we'd keep on bombing till the Japs surrendered, but, even though everybody was sure the war would end any minute, it wasn't till August fourteenth that we got the good news. At seven P.M., Truman announced it on the radio. The war was finally over.

I jumped up, yelling and cheering, but Grandma just sat there, staring at the radio. "Thanks be to God," she said. "I can't condone the bombing but I'm glad the fighting and killing are over at last."

"You're as bad as Stu," I said, but Grandma was looking at the picture of President Roosevelt hanging over the radio.

"If only he'd lived long enough to see this day," she said. "Who would have guessed the end would come without FDR?"

June leaned against Grandma's side. "Is the war over in California, too?"

"Of course, honey. I imagine your mother and father are as happy as we are."

"I wish they were here," June said, getting all teary-eyed and sad. Which goes to show our family could turn the happiest of times into the unhappiest. Here we'd finally won the war, and June was crying for Mama and Grandma was fretting about President Roosevelt and the atom bomb. Soon we'd all be boo-hoo-hooing.

It was Donny who saved the day. Bounding up the front steps, he opened the screen door and stepped into the hall. "Hey, June Bug," he called. "Come on outside. I've got a surprise for you and Gordy."

We followed him to the backyard. Pulling a handful of cherry bombs out of his pocket, he said, "I've been saving these for this moment."

Donny set them off, one after another. *Bam, bam, bam*—just like artillery fire. I begged him to let me light at least one but he said I might blow off a finger or something. It made me sore to be treated like a little kid so I watched all by myself from the porch steps. If William had been there, it might not have been so bad. We could have made jokes about Donny, called him names, teased him—things it's no fun to do by yourself.

I looked over at the Sullivans' house. A man was mowing the lawn. He came once a week to keep the yard in shape. When he saw me looking at him, he raised his hand and made a V for Victory sign. I grinned and made the sign to him. But I wished I knew where William was and what he was doing. And if he was ever coming back.

After Donny used up all his firecrackers, we could hear others popping and banging all over Grandville. It was better than the Fourth of July. Horns blew, church bells rang, the fire siren down by the train tracks blasted the All Clear. Inside, the radio played "When the Lights Go on Again All Over the World." A bunch of kids marched past the house wearing old Civil Defense helmets and waving little American flags. They were trying to sing "The Star-Spangled Banner" without much success.

When June saw her friend Nancy, she ran to join the parade, laughing and singing, Mama forgotten.

Donny sat down beside me and lit a cigarette. I was tempted to ask for a drag, but Grandma was watching from the doorway. Most likely Donny would have said no anyhow.

We talked for a while about the atom bomb. What might have happened if the Nazis had invented it first. What it must be like to see that mushroom cloud towering over your head. How it might change things forever.

Though I didn't tell Donny, the newspaper pictures of what the bomb had done scared me. We'd blasted Hiroshima flat. Miles and miles of rubble and twisted metal. People with their clothes and hair burned off. Some incinerated in a flash, the paper said. Lots of kids no bigger than my little brothers had been killed or injured. We'd done the same thing to Nagasaki. Like Grandma, I hoped nobody would drop that bomb on us.

When Donny and I ran out of things to say about the bomb, we drifted off into baseball. "Remember the time the old man took you and me and Stu down to Griffith Stadium to see the Senators play?" Donny asked.

I scowled. It was just like that trip to Ocean City he'd told me about. Why had all the good things happened when I was too little to remember them?

"You had a great time," Donny went on. "Stu carried you on his shoulders and some lady took your picture because she thought you were so cute." He laughed and tweaked my cheek.

I pulled away, mad. I didn't like being treated like a dumb little kid. "Well, I'm not cute anymore," I said.

"That's for sure," Donny agreed. "Man, you'd break that poor lady's camera if she aimed it at your ugly mug now." He laughed to show he was joking, and I laughed, too. Though I didn't really think it was all that funny.

Just when I thought Donny was going to stick around, he got to his feet. "Time to meet Charlie," he said.

"What are you and him going to do?" I asked. Even though I knew better, I wished he'd say they were going fishing or to play ball and I could go with them.

"What do you think?" Donny laughed. "Get loaded

and sleep it off tomorrow. Manny's closing for V-J Day."

After he left, Grandma came out and made herself comfortable beside me. "Sure is hot," she said.

I wiped the sweat off my forehead. My shirt stuck to my back and the waistband of my shorts was soaked through. "If it would just rain," I said.

Grandma sighed in agreement. "We could use it. The corn's drying up in the fields outside town."

We sat there for a few minutes, thinking our own thoughts. Finally Grandma asked where Donny had gone.

"Down to Fourth Street with Charlie McBride," I said. "They're celebrating the end of the war in some bar."

Grandma sighed. "I guess one excuse is as good as another." To my surprise, she put her arm around my shoulders and gave me a quick hug. "You miss William, don't you?"

I shrugged. "Do you think he'll ever come back?"

"Summer's almost over," Grandma said. "He's bound to come home soon."

"He'll probably still be mad at me."

"I doubt it, Gordy. By now, William probably realizes you didn't intend any harm."

"But I did," I muttered.

Grandma stared at me. "What do you mean?"

I felt my face heat up like an oven. "I got so mad at him down in the park that day—first because I thought he wasn't trying and then because he wouldn't do anything but cry and cuss and act like he hated me. I wanted to hit him, I wanted to beat him up. I almost did, too."

Afraid to look at Grandma, I clenched my fists and pounded my own knees. "I'm just like the old man," I said, itchy with shame. "Hitting people. Even people like William who can't fight back."

There. I'd said it. I'd told Grandma the worst thing about myself. Something much worse than cussing or smoking. I was sure she'd get up and go inside, maybe even call the reform school to come and get me. A boy who wanted to hit a crippled kid. I belonged in jail, all right.

"But you didn't hit him, did you?"

I stared at Grandma, surprised by her soft voice. Her eyes probed mine, seeking the truth.

"No," I said. "I didn't hit him, but it was all I could do to stop myself. I really wanted to."

"Well," Grandma said, "I think that says a lot about you, Gordy. You wanted to, but you didn't. That took strength of character, young man."

I couldn't think of anything to say, so she went on. "Look at it this way. Your father's been hitting you all your life, taking his temper out on you and your mother and your brothers and sister. It's all you've known, Gordy. Bullying people to make them do what you want."

Grandma put her arm around my shoulders and gave me another little hug. "Now it's up to you to learn a different way. Find out who you are. Follow your own footsteps, no one else's."

I studied my feet as if they might hold some clues as to where they planned to take me, but they were just their ordinary old dirty selves.

"There's a song we sing in school," I said slowly. "'This Land Is Your Land.' Do you know the one I mean?"

Grandma smiled and nodded. "I know it well."

"It has a part about roaming and rambling and following my footsteps. . . ."

Grandma began singing and I joined in. We sang about the redwood forest and the Gulf Stream waters, the ribbon of highway and the endless skyway, the golden valley and the sparkling sands of the diamond deserts. Then we just sat together, nice and quiet. Strange as it sounds, I actually enjoyed being with Grandma. Most grown-ups talk you to death or nag and carry on or cuss you out, but not her. She was peaceful to be with.

"Speaking of school," Grandma said, long after I'd forgotten mentioning it. "You'll be starting Orville Wright Junior High in a couple of weeks. Brand-new teachers, Gordy. A chance to make a fresh beginning."

She spoke cautiously, feeling her way along like a soldier in a minefield. She knew I hated school. Why had she gone and ruined everything by bringing the subject up?

"New teachers," I muttered, "but not new students. I'll still have to see Langerman's ugly face every day."

Grandma laughed. "Didn't I tell you the latest gossip?"

"No."

"Well, Mrs. Maxwell told me Dr. Langerman caught Jerry behind the garage sharing his best bourbon with a couple of other boys. His most expensive cigars, too. Havanas, Mrs. Maxwell said. Cost a fortune."

"I hope he whipped Langerman's tail," I said, picturing the scene.

"Better yet," Grandma said. "He's shipping him off to a military academy in Pennsylvania."

"Langerman's going up North? He'll be surrounded by damn Yankees." I started laughing. "He'll start the Civil War all over again—and probably lose it, too!"

Grandma chuckled. "I never liked that boy *or* his father." Getting to her feet, she said, "I'd best get dinner started. Why don't you hunt up June for me?"

I walked down to Nancy's house, still grinning to myself about Langerman. Without him around, I might find some guys to hang out with. Now that I'd ruined things with William, I could use a friend or two.

June was playing paper dolls on Nancy's front porch. When she saw me coming, she jumped up and ran to meet me. "Guess what, Gordy? Nancy's having a birthday party and I'm invited! She's having a big cake from the bakery and ice cream and pony rides!"

"That's great, June Bug."

June turned and waved good-bye to Nancy. "See you tomorrow," she called. To me, she said, "It's the first birthday party I've ever been invited to. I hope I know what to do."

I grinned at her. "You'll figure it out, June Bug. A smart cookie like you."

While June and I walked home, cars sped past us, horns honking, radios blaring, folks yelling out the windows. Firecrackers still banged and popped all over town. It seemed the whole country was happy tonight, including June and me.

Twenty-four

❖ ❖ ❖ ❖ ❖

A couple of nights later, I was sprawled on the living room floor listening to "Suspense" on the radio. It was scarier than usual. June huddled on the sofa with her hands over her ears, afraid to stay and listen, afraid to leave and miss what happened next.

Grandma came in from the kitchen and sat down beside her. "Silly," she whispered, putting her arm around her. "It's just a radio show, honey."

When the show's sponsor stopped the action for an advertisement, Grandma leaned toward me and said, "I have something to tell you, Gordy."

I looked up, scared it might be bad news, but she was smiling.

"The Sullivans are back," she said. "I just saw the car in the driveway."

I jumped up and ran to the window, practically knocking the screen out to get a look at the Sullivans' house. Sure enough, lights shone from the windows, including William's room.

"Can I go over there?" I was halfway out the door when Grandma called me back.

"Not tonight, Gordy," she said. "It's late and they're probably tired. Wait till tomorrow."

"But—"

"No buts," Grandma said in her strictest voice. "And no flashing lights in William's window either," she said as I started up the stairs. "That child needs his rest."

I flung myself down on the carpet. The commercial was over and the show was starting again. A door creaked open, somebody screamed, and June whimpered. Would the lady escape from the crazy man? Or would she join his other victims buried in the basement? That took my mind off William for a while.

At bedtime, Grandma made me promise not to disturb William. I stared at his window for a long time, hoping maybe he'd flash an SOS at me, but his room stayed dark and silent. If it hadn't been for the lights downstairs and the car in the driveway, I wouldn't have known William was back.

The next day, Grandma refused to let me go knock on William's door. She said I had to wait till I was invited.

"Remember," she said, "Mrs. Sullivan wasn't very pleased with you the last time she saw you. You'd best wait and see how she feels about you now."

I took a seat on the front porch, where I'd be in

plain sight, and tried to read a Captain Hornblower story in the new *Saturday Evening Post*. But it was hard to keep my mind on it.

June, Nancy, and some new girl named Linda were jumping rope on the front walk. "Bow to the captain, bow to the queen," June chanted. "Touch the bottom like a submarine." *Whap, whap, whap* went the rope against the concrete. *Squeal, squeal, squeal* went the girls.

Above the racket they were making, I heard someone call my name. I looked up and there was William, standing at the gate grinning at me.

I tore down the front walk, messing up the jump-rope game, and skidded to a stop in front of him. This close, I realized he wasn't standing all by himself. Like a veteran home from the war, he had crutches fitted to his arms and braces on his legs, but he was on his feet, looking straight across at me for the first time.

Neither one of us said anything for a minute. We just stood there grinning like idiots.

"You're walking," I whispered. Then I let out a whoop and yelled, "You're walking, William! I knew you could!"

William's grin got wider and wider. "Not exactly," he said. "I can't stand up without crutches, but I'm getting stronger every day."

The noise we were making got June's attention. Dropping the jump rope, she came running to see what was going on. Nancy and Linda were right behind her.

"You're the boy with polio," Nancy said, her eyes wide. "I thought you couldn't walk."

"Do those things on your legs hurt?" Linda asked.

"Can I try your crutches sometime?" June asked.

"Go on," I said, "get out of here, you little monsters. Scram!"

The girls scattered, giggling.

As soon as they were gone, I started asking William *my* questions. "Were you really at your aunt's house all summer? How come you didn't send me a postcard or tell me when you were coming home? Why didn't you let me know you were learning to walk? Did you—"

"Lord, Gordy," William broke in. "Don't ask so many questions. You're giving me a headache."

"You're not still sore at me, are you?"

"Of course not. Why, in some ways, I have you to thank for this. If you hadn't taken me down to the park that day, Mother might never have gotten the idea to go to the special polio hospital in Minnesota."

"That's where you've been? All the way to Minnesota? William, that's more than halfway across America. How did you get there?"

"On the train."

I sighed, remembering the passenger trains that sped through College Hill. "You lucky duck. I bet you slept in a Pullman, didn't you? And ate fancy dinners and rode in one of those observation cars with a glass roof?"

Ignoring my questions about the train, William went on talking about the place he'd gone to. "The doctors told Mother I wasn't as bad off as she thought. They said she's been overprotecting me."

I grinned to myself. I could have told William *that* and not charged him one red cent, either.

"The doctors claim all I need is a little encouragement, plus lots of therapy and hard work." William paused a moment and looked me hard in the eye. "If I keep at it, Gordy, I might be walking all by myself next summer."

I hollered so loud my voice bounced back from the house across the street. "That's great, William, that's great!" I shouted, letting my mind race ahead, picturing the fun we'd have. First of all, I'd get a bike like the one in his garage. We'd pack lunches, go down in the woods across the train tracks, build a hut, start a gang—

"William," Mrs. Sullivan called from his front porch. "Better come in now. You mustn't tire yourself on your first day home."

"Come with me," William said. "One of my cousins gave me his old Erector set. It's all metal, made before the war. The kind you can't get nowadays."

I took a quick look at Mrs. Sullivan, but I couldn't decide if she was glaring at me or just squinting because the sun was in her eyes. "How about your mother?" I asked. "Is she still mad at me?"

William shook his head. "I don't think so."

Hoping he was right, I started toward his house, matching my steps to his. Walking was hard work for William. He winced sometimes, and his knuckles were white from gripping the crutches, but he swung himself along, doing his best to move his feet. Once or twice I reached out to steady him, but he shook his head. "I have to do it myself," he said, clenching his teeth.

When we reached the porch, Mrs. Sullivan said hello to me and asked if I'd had a nice summer. "Are you all ready for school, Gordon?"

"Yes, ma'am," I said, hating to be reminded that prison opened in three weeks.

"Isn't it wonderful to see William up on his feet?"

"Yes, ma'am, it sure is."

Luckily Mrs. Sullivan decided to quit talking after that. It was a strain for both of us to be so polite to each other.

Once we were upstairs in William's room, it was almost as if he'd never been away. While we fooled around with the Erector set, I told William about the old man's return. I figured he'd hear his mother's version soon enough. He might as well know what really happened.

William listened to the whole story without saying a word. Just sat there, eyes wide, taking in the details. When I got to the end, he said, "Your mother didn't even say good-bye?"

"Nope." Trying to fit two pieces of metal together, I jabbed my thumb. It started to bleed so I stuck it in my mouth to make it stop.

"You must feel terrible," William said.

I shrugged. "Mama and I never did get along too good."

Without any warning, a big hole opened up inside

me, and before I could stop myself I fell straight down to the bottom. I tried to turn off the waterworks, but tears shot out of my eyes like rain after a dry spell. It seemed I'd been fighting them for weeks and today I'd lost the battle.

William reached out and patted my shoulder. "I'm sorry, Gordy," he said.

I almost yelled at him to leave me alone, but I was blubbering too hard to talk. I don't know how long it took me to pull myself together, but when I'd finally stopped crying, I wiped my eyes on my shirttail and glared at William.

"If you ever say a word about me bawling," I said, "I'll hit you so hard you won't come down to earth for a year." As soon as the threat left my mouth I was sorry, but William just nodded as though he understood.

"I swear I'll never tell a soul," he said, crossing his heart.

"You better keep your promise," I muttered, "because I sure don't want to hit you."

"Don't worry," William said solemnly, "you and I are friends, Gordy. And friends don't betray each other."

"You talk just like a book sometimes," I said, teasing him so he wouldn't notice how glad I was he'd said we were friends.

William picked up a curved Erector piece. "See this? If we find more like it, I bet we could build the Eiffel Tower."

We hunted through the pieces, separating them into

piles according to their shape and size. When we had enough of the curved ones, William started building the base. He worked quickly, fitting things neatly together. I sat back on my heels and watched the tower take shape. William was better with the Erector pieces than I was, just as he was better at building model planes. He had more patience.

By the time Mrs. Sullivan came upstairs to check on us, William had almost finished the tower. "See what Gordy and I built, Mother?"

"Very nice," she said, bending down to kiss the top of William's head. "Is it the Eiffel Tower?"

William nodded and pulled away, his face red. I guess he was embarrassed, but I couldn't help wondering what it would be like to have a mother who did mushy things like that. Mama had never kissed me. Unless it was way back when I was Bobby's size and I just couldn't remember—like the vacation in Ocean City and the trip to Griffith Stadium. It seemed to me good things were easier to forget than bad things.

"I guess I'll go on home," I said, thinking I'd say it before Mrs. Sullivan had a chance to tell me to scram.

"Come back tomorrow, Gordon," Mrs. Sullivan said. "You and William might want to build the Empire State Building next."

"Good idea," William said, grinning at me.

I nodded, too surprised to say anything. Impossible as it seemed, Mrs. Sullivan sounded almost friendly.

Jumping to my feet, I said good-bye and ran down the stairs. Out the door I went, across the lawn, and over the fence to Grandma's yard. I could hardly wait to tell her about William. If I knew her, she'd be just as excited as I was.

As soon as I came through the front door, I smelled dinner cooking. Ham, I guessed, and apple pie for dessert. In the dining room, June was setting the table for four, which meant Donny would be joining us when he got off work. She laid the forks, knives, and spoons down carefully, lining them up just right.

Out in the kitchen, I heard Grandma singing "This Land Is Your Land." She was really belting it out, putting her whole heart into it.

"Hey, Grandma," I shouted, "I'm home!"

And do you know what? It was true. I was home. And happy to be there.

8543